W9-AER-696

PASSING THE WORD

WORD

Writers on Their Mentors

EDITED BY
Jeffrey Skinner & Lee Martin

Sarabande Books

LOUISVILLE, KENTUCKY

Managing Editor
Sarabande Books, Inc.
2234 Dundee Road, Suite 200
Louisville, KY 40205

LIBRARY OF CONGRESS CATALOGING-IN-PUBLICATION DATA

Passing the word : writers on their mentors / edited by Lee Martin and Jeffrey Skinner.
p.   cm.
ISBN 1-889330-59-0 (alk. paper)
1. Authors, American—20th century—Biography. 2. Authorship.
3. Mentoring of authors—United States. 4. Creative writing—Study and teaching—United States—History.   I. Martin, Lee, 1955- II. Skinner, Jeffrey.
PS129 P37 2001
810.9'0054—dc21   00-048240

Cover painting: *The Messengers* by Rodney Hatfield, used by permission of the artist

Cover and text design by Charles Casey Martin

Manufactured in the United States of America
This book is printed on acid-free paper.

Sarabande Books is a nonprofit literary organization.

Publication of this book was funded in part by a grant from the Kentucky Arts Council, a state agency of the Education, Arts and Humanities Cabinet, and by a grant from the National Endowment for the Arts.

FIRST EDITION

CONTENTS

PREFACE

I ENROLLED IN MY FIRST creative writing class in 1978 when I was an undergraduate at Eastern Illinois University. I was young, and I knew that I wanted to be a writer. I had no idea, however, what that meant. I didn't know what it meant to apprentice myself to a craft, to choose writing as a way of life, to open myself to the influence of mentors. My teacher was a man named Allen Neff. He would be my teacher for only a few days, but his presence and his eventual absence would be necessary to my first and most lasting lesson as a writer. When he entered our classroom that first day, I didn't know that he was ill with cancer, or that within a matter of weeks he would be dead.

When he finally became too ill to teach, his replacement, Asa Baber, gave us the full story. He told us that Allen was ill, that he spent his days in bed, cared for by colleagues and former students who read to him from his favorite books. Asa reached into his briefcase and pulled out a writing tablet, the sort that schoolchildren use when learning cursive handwriting, and a box of crayons. He suggested that Allen would appreciate it if we would send him our good wishes, if we would make the sorts of "cards" that we had once made our grade-school classmates who were ill. "Draw pictures," he told us. "Write whatever you feel."

So one of my initial assignments as a writer was to write a message to a man I barely knew, a man who was dying. I don't recall the message I wrote, nor the picture that I drew. I imagine it was a glowing orange sun with rays spiking out around its circumference. What I've never forgotten, though, is the awkward feel of the crayon in my hand, the messy lines and blurry words I left on the paper, that and how inadequate I felt, how humbled. My first lesson as a writer was a lesson in humanity, in connection, in speaking from the heart.

How could I find genuine words that would matter to a man who was dying?

Now, twenty-two years later, I teach in the creative writing program at the University of North Texas, where I also edit the *American Literary Review*. Like so many writers of the so-called "baby boom" generation—those writers born after World War II—I've learned my craft and passed on what I've learned within university writing communities. When Jeff Skinner and I set out to compile *Passing the Word: Writers on Their Mentors*, we merely wanted to collect some of the finest fiction and poetry being written today and to encourage these writers to speak of their mentors' influences. It turned out that these mentoring relationships often developed in university writing programs. So even though it wasn't our intention to cast any particular focus on creative writing programs, it is impossible to look at this anthology without making note of the fact that these programs have become America's literary salons. Writers have always sought out other writers, and, as the following pages illustrate, many of the writers in this country since World War II have done so in university creative writing workshops. Still, as Jeff points out in his essay which follows, what stands out most prominently in the writers' essays that we've paired with their own stories and poems is the individual give and take between apprentice writers and their mentors.

The idea for *Passing the Word* came about as a result of a special *American Literary Review* issue that we published in the spring of 1999. To celebrate *ALR*'s tenth anniversary, we decided to devote an issue to the best writing that we could gather from faculty at creative writing programs and their students. We hoped that such an issue would mark the passage of time by evoking past, present, and future distinction. Jeff Skinner was one of the writing teachers included in that issue and, shortly after its appearance, he proposed an anthology of similar ilk—a book that would not only be a collection of outstanding contemporary poetry and fiction, but also a gathering of writers' essays that, together, would give readers a deeper understanding of craft and how any one writer's development is dependent on the relationship he or she has with a particular mentor or group of mentors.

We set out to cast as wide of a net as possible, tendering invitations to writers who came from diverse backgrounds and experiences, but all of the same post–World War II group. Some of the writers in *Passing the Word* published their first books as early as 1975; others have published first books as recently as 1994. Jeff and I thought that such a group of writers would have some interesting things to say about their mentors, who would be, of course, writers from the preceding generation. In the process, we would get a sense of the creative writing movement in America following World War II.

Our strategy has produced exactly that. The essays that follow give an excellent sense of one generation of writers "passing the word" to another generation. But, as with all strategies, ours has brought to light certain accurate, yet unfortunate, characteristics. Chief among these is the unbalanced gender and racial representation among the mentors acknowledged in this anthology. We wish this could be otherwise, but we also have to accept the historical statement that such an inequity makes: In the early years of creative writing instruction in this country, the teachers were overwhelmingly white and male. This fact is, of course, changing as new, more diverse, generations of writers arrive on the scene.

The assembly of writers that we've collected in *Passing the Word* acknowledge the influences of those who help the writer along, who read and comment, and nurture and encourage. As Jeff and I have gathered these essays, I've thought often of my teacher, Allen Neff, lying on his deathbed, listening to the sounds of his former students' voices, reading to him words he had long loved.

All of the essays contained here demonstrate that although the literal act of putting words on the page is a solitary activity, no writer is ever alone. There are always those mentors, those students, who engage in a communal effort of creation. The result is evident in the wonderful work that each of these writers has contributed, work that becomes a mentoring influence for those writers, no matter how far along in their careers, who read it, who go on to their own creations. The cycle of teaching and learning spins on; the word is passed, and we are all the better.

—*Lee Martin*

INTRODUCTION
The Scrupulous Philanthropy of Expertise

ROBERT AITKEN, WHO HAS PRACTICED and taught Zen in America since 1959, has this to say about mentors: "The good teacher is necessary for two reasons. She or he will encourage you and offer you guidance. She or he will also deny you the complacency of a plateau and urge you on to the peak of your potential and even beyond."

What's being "taught" in this instance is, at bottom, the path to satori or enlightenment, a notoriously ineffable, dynamic state of sudden awakening. Zen teachers have always sternly cautioned their students in this quest against reliance on words, which may lead to substituting abstraction for direct experience. But it's hard to think of any other spiritual discipline that has resulted in more sheer volume of words—poetry and prose—than have been published under the banner of Zen. The quote from Roshi Aitken, for example, is taken from his ninth published book.

This paradox is only one of many encountered in Zen study. At the risk of hubris (or heresy), I think it serves as useful analog to the contradictions and paradoxes one finds in *Passing the Word*. Indeed, the question, "Can creative writing be taught?" is a kind of secular "koan" enacted daily in the hundreds of creative writing programs across the country. It is a question that has been endlessly debated in various forums. But in the end the important answers, such as they are, arise in one-on-one transaction between writing teacher and student. Lee Martin and I saw a need for a more direct presentation of this process, a gathering of testimony on the experiential particulars of mentoring. *Something* is being taught, and learned, in these "conferences," each one itself a paradoxical blend of institutionalized ritual and intimate informality. It is that *something* that the essays in *Passing the Word* address, and go a good way toward defining.

As in Zen, teaching methods in creative writing often seem to issue from the personality and temperament of the teacher, and can sometimes look capricious and illogical. It is a practice with no agreed-upon handbook or instruction manual; it is clearly more than a matter of the transmission of craft, technique, information. The student wants something the master has. But what? He wants to submit to superior knowledge, practice, and position, but where is the line between submission and erasure of self?

"Mentoring is a complicated business," David Wojahn says, "because it is conducted always in a state of unease. The disciple wants to be changed by the mentor, changed utterly. And yet the self is more likely to resist such change than to welcome it." Some of the authors in this anthology speak openly of this ambiguous drive. Reginald Shepherd provides an explicit (and powerful) psychological cause for his resistance: "In my experience those in a position to be mentors want to break you and remake you, if not in their own image, then in their image of who or what you should be.... Perhaps because I lived for seven years with a vicious stepfather who was determined to break me (he broke my mother: she died), I've never had much taste for being broken...."

Sometimes the student, who generally comes to writing with an undeveloped, nebulous notion of what her "self" *is*, needs contact with disparate sorts of mentors in order to test and clarify the competing forces within. In her essay, Maura Stanton speaks of two very different mentoring experiences: "I approached Berryman and told him I wrote poetry, too. His breath flamed. His hand clawed at my arm. I could see his reddened eyes behind the thick black glasses. Writing poetry was a miserable business, he said." Then, in very dissimilar terms, she speaks of her study with another poet: "I blossomed as a poet under Vern's mild, gentle praise and unobtrusive suggestions." Stanton makes clear that she felt an inarticulate but urgent need for contact with *both* teachers: "All that winter I went back and forth between John Berryman and Vern Rutsula, frightened by one, reassured by the other."

The encouragement and guidance Aitken asserts are part of the necessity of a good teacher show up repeatedly in these essays. Over and over we hear the tone of epiphanic surprise experienced by students when their teachers treat their halting, unformed work with serious attention. Of William Meredith, Michael Collier says, "In the classroom he treated all of our various motives, ambitions, and pretensions with seriousness and candor." "I was only nineteen," Elizabeth Graver says of her encounter with Annie Dillard, "but Annie took me (and all her students) utterly seriously as a writer, and so conveyed to me that I should take myself seriously, too...." What many former students remember of their teachers is the sheer time and energy they devoted to apprentice work. "Confronting one of my particularly messy stories," Erin McGraw says of her teacher John L'Heureux, "he made an outline, blocking out each scene (thirteen of them in sixteen pages) and showing where it went. Mostly, nowhere." The rueful humor of McGraw's last sentence is retrospective; it underlines the transformative power of a teacher's attention to student work in the process of revision. The teacher, after all, has been there, and learned the hard lesson of perseverance, in the face of uncertain outcome.

Such small moments of precise, focused attention on the writing—the words themselves in all their particularity—can be unforgettable lessons. Jay McInerney relates one session with Ray Carver, in which "we spent some ten or fifteen minutes debating my use of the word 'earth.' Carver felt it had to be 'ground,' and he felt it was worth the trouble of talking it through. That one exchange was invaluable; I think of it constantly when I'm working."

In conjunction with this kind of micro-counsel, what many

students take from mentors is a more global orientation toward writing, a generalized stance that becomes the ground for future work. "It was Dorothy Vella who taught me that writing is seeing," Sylvia Wantanabe says, mixing gratitude and a directness reminiscent of her mentor. The "push" of a teacher often becomes encapsulated in aphorism, which the student carries into his own writing—"...he repeated a claim for poetry I remembered him making frequently," Michael Collier says of William Meredith: "'Poetry and experience should have an exact ratio.'" The palpable affection of Dana Gioia's portrait of Elizabeth Bishop demonstrates the subtle, implicit, and lasting effect a good teacher can have on her student: "She never articulated her philosophy in class, but she practiced it so consistently that it is easy—especially now, a decade later—to see what she was doing. She wanted us to see poems, not ideas...."

Aitken's second reason for the necessity of a good teacher—"She or he will also deny you the complacency of a plateau and urge you on to the peak of your potential and even beyond"—is borne out quite explicitly in the essays of *Passing the Word*. Erin McGraw describes this painful gauntlet: "Even when I felt stung and underappreciated—pretty much every week—I had a dim sense that John was driving me toward a specific goal, and his goal was bigger and better than any I had constructed for myself." And even Reginald Shepard, who begins his essay with a severely skeptical caveat on the value of mentors in general, recognizes that the one man he can call his mentor, Alvin Feinman, "never 'did anything' for me but help me write better poems; he never did anything *to* me but force me to see that however pleased I was with something I'd just written, it could always be better, *had* to be better if I was to call myself a poet." This raising of the bar, far above what the student thought necessary or possible, is a theme common to the recollections in our anthology. It seems part and parcel of the seriousness (it should be pointed out that many authors note a teacher's admonition to also retain a sense of play in the writing) with which mentors approach both the art of writing in general and the student's particular efforts.

The passionate discipline mentors bring to the art is a contagious attitude, at least for those students who come bearing their own gifted desire. In this sense the evidence of *Passing the Word* would suggest that the mentor/student relationship is a collaboration—one of shared intensity—directed toward the practice of perhaps the most difficult and elusive of all the arts. Humility before the vastness of language, entered into with a combination of fear and love, is a democratizing *process*, whether one is making the journey for the first, or the five-hundredth time. Because of the intimidating potential of the medium, and the long gorgeous shadows cast by illustrious predecessors, a guide can make all the difference. Perhaps this is why these essays so often seem permeated with the bittersweet tang of homage. Even students age, after all. Teachers die. Students themselves become mentors to others, and the cycle begins again. Through it all, writing continues. "I've come to think of him as Peter rather than Mr. Taylor," David Huddle writes. "Probably it's because I'm older now than he was then—it's as if I've aged into peer status with him."

Discipline, humility, kindness. These qualities cohere in the best mentors, bundled into an overarching approach to the art of writing. It is not, I think, coincidence that the writers in this collection remember these qualities best when speaking of their mentors as *people*, as fellow pilgrims who helped them on the way. In some sense, whether consciously or not, we seek out mentors to learn how to live—as an artist, and as a human being. And whether we learn a little or a great deal about the craft of writing from our mentor, we will likely retain something of their demonstration of being in the world. "Yet it is kindness such as Jim displayed," David Wojahn writes, "this scrupulous philanthropy of expertise, which counted the most in our relationship, more so, I think, than the actual usefulness of his advice."

—*Jeffrey Skinner*

Michael Collier

MICHAEL COLLIER has published three collections of poetry, *The Clasp and Other Poems*, *The Folded Heart*, and *The Neighbor*. In addition he has edited three highly acclaimed anthologies, *The Wesleyan Tradition: Four Decades of Contemporary American Poetry*, *The New Bread Loaf Anthology of Contemporary American Poetry* (coedited with Stanley Plumly), and *The New American Poets: A Bread Loaf Anthology*. He has received a Pushcart Prize, two National Endowment for the Arts fellowships, a Guggenheim fellowship, the Alice Fay di Castagnola Prize from the Poetry Society of America, and a "Discovery"/*The Nation* Award.

An Exact Ratio

>>>>>>>>>>>>>>>>>>>>><<<<<<<<<<<<<<<

In 1971 as a freshman at a California college I did not want to be attending, I thought my misplacement could be cured by seeking out John Berryman or Robert Lowell, two poets I was devoted to. By the time I got around to acting on this impulse, Berryman had committed suicide, and Robert Lowell, I discovered, was living in England. My encounters with their work, however, had led me to many other poets, including William Meredith. I took notice that Berryman dedicated more "Dream Songs" to Meredith than anyone else, and excerpts from Meredith's reviews of Lowell graced that poet's dust jackets. For Meredith's own *Earth Walk: New and Selected Poems*, Lowell had written: "Meredith is an expert writer and knows how to make his meters and sentences accomplish hard labors. His intelligent poems, unlike most poems, have character behind them." The photograph of Meredith from *Earth Walk* showed a man nothing like the poets I imagined I might study with. Instead of a shaggy and bearded Berryman among Irish ruins or the bushwhacked countenance of Lowell in Berg's and Mezey's *Naked Poetry*, Meredith in stark contrast maintained a civic face: handsome, full, and solid.

In August of 1972, before leaving to study in England for a semester, I spent two weeks hitchhiking through New England, visiting schools I thought I might transfer to the following year. I had learned from his book jacket that Meredith taught at Connecticut College. And so on an oppressively humid day, shortly after the massacre of the Israeli Olympic team members in Munich, I arrived in New London. It was lunch hour when I got to the college's admissions office where only one person was on duty. Fortunately, she had seen Meredith earlier in the day. She urged me to find him before he went home and showed me the way to the Thames Hall, where the English Department was housed. I encountered Meredith negotiating a narrow back staircase. He was struggling with a standard Remington typewriter and now was forced to cradle it uncomfortably as I explained myself from a few steps below. There was no air-conditioning in the building, and the humidity was not only suffocating but it possessed the deep vacant emptiness of a school building in hibernation. Meredith realized soon I was a situation that couldn't be dealt with in the stairway. He suggested we talk in his office.

William Meredith was the first poet I had ever met and to find him weighted with a typewriter, his face pricked with perspiration, his manner so like the manner of other mortals I knew, startled me with familiarity and shocked me into my first glimpse of the truth that a poem or any art always begins with a particular man or woman. This particular man, William Meredith, was nothing like the person in the book jacket portrait. He had ragged, longish gray hair, combed straight back and tucked behind his ears where it curled up from under the lobes. He had respectably fashionable sideburns. His eyes had large blue irises, the kind of blue you see in Chinese porcelain. He wore a blue, open-collar shirt and flared-bottom chinos. His feet were bracketed by sandals. The most distinctive thing about him was his face. It was really two faces, like halves of the moon in different phases. I wondered if he had suffered a stroke that had left one side partially paralyzed. He listened courteously to me and at one point pulled out the typing leaf from his desk on which he propped his feet.

Out of my infatuations with Berryman and Lowell, I had constructed a tenderfoot's map of contemporary American poetry. It led me by way of uncritical association to think of Meredith as a confessional poet. About this I couldn't have been more wrong. Meredith, I would discover, loved the work of Berryman and Lowell, but he loved the particular men and their difficult struggles more. One of the things I would learn from Meredith was that a poet's work was not merely an expression of his experience, but that it was interesting and intriguing, and necessary, to the degree in which it enacted a struggle between the private and public, the personal and impersonal. He often cited Berryman's essay "The Development of Anne Frank" and one of his favorite contemporary poems was Jack Gilbert's "The Abnormal Is Not Courage." Meredith begins a memoir about W. H. Auden by quoting the poet Louise Coxe, a Princeton roommate of Meredith's, who called Auden, "So public a private man."

When I started Connecticut College in the fall of 1973, Meredith was finishing the persona sequence *Hazard, the Painter*. In the most reductive terms it is an optimist's response to the dark times that yielded the suicides of Plath, Jarrell, Berryman, and Sexton, and the politics of Vietnam and Watergate. In the poem, Meredith has put an alter-ego, Hazard, "in charge of morale in a morbid time." In *Hazard* and the poems that were to follow, until his silencing stroke in 1983, his overriding concern is morale. In "In Loving Memory of the Late Author of Dream Songs," Meredith defined the peculiar nature of this morale and his preoccupation with it:

Morale is what I think about all the time
now, what hopeful men and women can say and do.
But having to speak for you, I can't
lie. 'Let his giant faults appear, as sent
together with his virtues down,' the song says.

It says suicide is a crime
and that wives and children deserve better than this.
None of us deserved, of course, you.

Do we wave back now, or what do we do?
You were never reluctant to instruct.
I do what's in character, I look for things
to praise on the riverbanks and I praise them.
We are all relicts, of some great joy, wearing black,
but this book is full of marvelous songs.
Don't let us contract your dread recidivism
and start falling from our own iron railings.
Wave from the fat book again, make us wave back.

Morale and optimism were not fashionable notions to be touting in the seventies and early eighties, and Meredith knew it. He was acutely aware that morale and morality, praising and preaching, can be easily and even willfully confused. "Temperament" was a word he liked to use when describing the imperatives one lives by. Our temperaments were to be discovered as examples of human response. They were transcendental features of one's character. Character did not suggest balance and stability and harmony but rather the arena where the public and private parts of one's self might negotiate the terms of an existence.

I wanted the drama of Berryman and Lowell, the fire-breathingness and on-the-edgeness-of-things they represented and not the responsible struggle of Meredith's cause. Initially, it was hard for me as his student to take in what he was saying, though through the rigor and beauty, the fair arguments enacted in his poems, I could hear its frequencies. Also, the example of his generosity, his willingness to include others in many aspects of his life, was as disarming as it was instructive. Meredith himself was his own best argument for optimism and hope. In the classroom he treated all of our various motives, ambitions, and pretensions with seriousness and candor. Very little time was spent editing the stories and poems we brought to class. Meredith was more interested in approaching our work, any work, in order to get at the source of what he might call its original insight or particular response to experience. He drew on the tradition of English poetry, especially the Romantics, not in any scholarly or esoteric way, but in a way that allowed us to see how we struggle to make sense of life through art. In 1983, I sat in on an interview conducted by *The Paris Review* with him. In response to a question about his relatively low output of six poems per year, he said, "I wait until the poems seem to be addressed not to 'Occupant' but to 'William Meredith.'" And he repeated a claim for poetry I remembered him making frequently when I was a student: "Poetry and experience should have an exact ratio." As a teacher he was interested in getting his students to see that our jobs, not just as writers, but as men and women, were to avoid the default status of "Occupant."

Since I was determined to become a writer and unerringly if not prematurely thought myself one, and since I had traveled physically and culturally, from California and Arizona, so far to cultivate my vocation, I was constantly crossing the threshold of his office. I know I must have been awkwardly persistent and to other students a hog for his time and attention. And since I had declared my intentions so early to Meredith, I must have assumed he knew what my expectations were, regardless of my talents. Whatever awkwardness obtained because of my urgencies, Meredith negotiated it easily and very soon had taken me on unconditionally. On a number of occasions I was invited to informal dinners at his house or to accompany him to readings at nearby Wesleyan and Yale. Once he asked me to drive him in his car to a reading at St. Michael's College in Winooski, Vermont. He was serving a term as secretary for the American Academy and National Institutes of Arts and Letters and wanted to use the time in the car to work on citations for the recipients of that year's awards. We had got off to a late start, but for the first couple hours I kept to the 55-mile-per-hour speed limit. After all, I was driving my distinguished teacher's car, a faded, hand-me-down Cadillac, a gift from his stepmother no less! At one point Meredith broke from his work, leaned over so he could see the speedometer, and then looked outside the window. With this information he calculated I would not deliver him to Winooski in time. "I'll pay for the ticket," he reassured me. As the car responded to his hint, he returned calmly to his citations. But most of the times I accompanied Mr. Meredith, which is what I called him until my day of graduation when he asked me to stop, he was the chauffeur. He liked to engage whoever he was with in conversation about things they knew that he might not. I could talk about the desert. For his part, he tried his best to teach me about the trees and creatures of New England. I remember learning about the delicate blossoms of the shadblow tree and how Frost had accurately portrayed the ovenbird in his poem of that title.

Meredith himself had accompanied Robert Frost on Frost's last reading trip to California, in 1961. They took the train. One night several days into the journey, they quarreled. I can't remember if Frost lost his temper with Meredith, or if it was the other way around. But the upshot was that Frost was the one who tried to patch things up by telling him, "I brought you along on this trip so you could see a little how I take myself." Meredith liked to say with regard to that incident that a definition of style "is how a man takes himself." As a teacher and later a friend what I learned most consistently from William Meredith was that he took himself both seriously and playfully. He preferred directness over coyness; self-effacement over self-aggrandizement. He was, to rephrase his poem, a relict of some great joy who refused to wear black.

During spring break of 1975, I attended a reading he gave with

X. J. Kennedy at the New School. Daniel Halpern, who had arranged the reading, introduced the poets. He also informed us that Charles Wright and Mark Strand were in the audience. These were poets I was just finding my way to and was excited to see them in the flesh. After the reading Meredith suggested I come along with everyone to dinner. There were a number of other guests as well, including his sister Kay, and Grace Schulman, as well as Wright, Strand, Halpern, and a staff member of Halpern's at *Antaeus*.

At dinner there was talk about Eugenio Montale having recently been given the Nobel Prize for Literature. Someone reported that one of Montale's responses to the award was, "In a life of mostly unhappiness, this makes it a little less unhappy," or so I remember. Montale's words brought vocal and head-shaking approval from different parts of the table. But from Meredith there was silence, uncomfortable, ruminating silence that soon turned to argumentative disapproval. He couldn't understand what there was to praise in Montale's attitude toward the prize and life. He argued that our obligation as writers was to speak against the despair, "fashionable despair" is the phrase he used, characterized by Montale. Everyone had had a lot of wine and Meredith had been drinking vodka. There was a kind of squaring off between him and a few others, while most, after making feeble mediating gestures, remained neutral, though ill at ease. After a while there was a cessation of hostilities, but even so it was difficult to continue with dinner. Meredith's quarrel, of course, wasn't with Montale or even with the people at dinner; it was with a culture that no longer valued the poet as the singer of its tribe's songs, and the realization that the values he honored were no longer prized. Nevertheless, he wasn't going to accept the shift from hope to despair that he believed had taken place all around him. A few hours earlier he had used his alter-ego Hazard to state his case:

Gnawed by a vision of rightness
that no one else seems to see,
what can a man do
But bear witness?

And what has he got to tell?
Only the shaped things he's seen—
a few things made by men
a galaxy made well.

Though more of each day is dark,
though he's awkward at the job,
he squeezes paint from a tube.
Hazard is back at work.

If Frost had brought Meredith along to see how he took himself, Meredith had provided me with a similar opportunity that night. What I witnessed in Meredith's argument at dinner was how conviction can distort a man's style. The usually decorous and chivalrous citizen-poet who used form and convention—social and artistic—to harness his powerful feelings and emotions allowed me to see what the feelings themselves might be like. Perhaps most of the people at the dinner thought Meredith wrongheaded and quarrelsome, but what I saw, as his student, was an act of courage. It was courage lacking finesse, perhaps, but courage nevertheless. It was a hidden aspect of Meredith's character, one that might get overlooked because of his fastidious manners. I think this courage was what Lowell saw in Meredith's poems, what was "behind them."

In 1975, I could not have known how long my association with William Meredith would last. At some point students and mentors often enact a struggle usually born of the student's need to create his own identity. But that has never happened between us. In 1983, Meredith had a stroke, when he was only sixty-four, that has left him expressively aphasic—virtually unable to speak but thoroughly capable of understanding. Although I have missed—mourned, really—the poems he has not been able to write during the last two decades, I have never been without his example of courage, in the form of his character. Character is probably even less fashionable to talk about today than it was in the seventies. When we do we might hear it described as a form of personality infrastructure or the hardwired components of the self. Generally, our attitude is that it's inherited or determined by the times we live in. Meredith's point, however, was that you cultivate it and use it like artistic form to resist solipsism and morbidity. Character gets tested during difficult times. In fact, that's its purpose.

I see William Meredith three or four times each year. Each time I'm in his presence I experience the original feeling of privilege I had when I first met him almost thirty years ago. Although his speaking ability is very much diminished, his spirit is as present and active as ever. He does not shy from argument, especially when he feels called to counter the dark and despairing forces of human nature. And he does spare his former student criticism. Not too many years ago I was extolling the virtues of the English painter Francis Bacon to the painter Emily Maxwell. Meredith was in the room with us, listening intently with his handsome divided face and blue eyes. I could tell he wanted to get into the discussion but was searching for the words. Finally, they burst out of him clear and true and in character, "But so what!" he declared, "Bacon, unhappy man!"

The Farrier

The book is in my hands then his.
The desk, the lamp, the carpet fragment,
the pictures of the poets on the wall,
and then the window, and out beyond
the window, the land drops off steeply
to the river. The river winds into the sound
and the sound into the ocean. The book
we are reading is not the thing we pass
between us. The book we are reading
has not been written. It won't contain
"The Poem of Two Friends." It won't be called
"Teacher & Student," even now that one of us
is old, the other idling fluidly in middle age:
the book won't be written.
So how will we sort
the hammer and tongs? Who will wear
the bright bandanna around his head
or forge the useless shoe?
What is the sound the anvil
no longer makes?
The worked iron
cools in its own steam. It's night
beyond the window. Inside, the light
is bright enough for reading.
A mist spreads upward from the river.
The book is in his hand then mine.

for William Meredith

Jay McInerney

JAY MCINERNEY debuted with the novel *Bright Lights, Big City*, which documents the coming-of-age excesses of New York City life in the 1980s and later was made into a major motion picture starring Michael J. Fox. He followed with the novels *Ransom, Story of My Life, The Last of the Savages*, and the novella *Model Behavior*, an insider's look at the glamorous world of fashion. His journalism has appeared in *The New Yorker, Vanity Fair*, and *Esquire*, among many other places. Married with children, he divides his time between New York and Tennessee.

Raymond Carver:
A Still, Small Voice

>>>>>>>>>>>>>>>>>>>>>>X<<<<<<<<<<<<<<<<<<<<

A year after his death, the recurring image I associate with Raymond Carver is one of people leaning toward him, working very hard at the act of listening. He mumbled. T. S. Eliot once described Ezra Pound, qua mentor, as "a man trying to convey to a very deaf person the fact that the house is on fire." Raymond Carver had precisely the opposite manner. The smoke could be filling the room, flames streaking across the carpet, before Carver would ask, "Is it, uh, getting a little hot in here, maybe?" And you would be sitting in your chair, bent achingly forward at the waist, saying, "Beg pardon, Ray?" Never insisting, rarely asserting, he was an unlikely teacher. I once sat in and listened while Carver was interviewed for two and a half hours. The writer conducting the interview moved the tape recorder closer and closer and finally asked if Carver would put it in his lap. A few days later the interviewer called up, near despair: Ray's voice on the tapes was nearly inaudible. The word "soft-spoken" hardly begins to do justice to his speech; this condition was aggravated whenever he was pressed into the regions of generality or prescription.

As I say, he mumbled, and if it once seemed merely a physical tic, akin to cracking knuckles or the drumming of a foot, I now think it was a function of a deep humility and a respect for the language bordering on awe, a reflection of his sense that words should be handled very, very gingerly. As if it might be almost impossible to say what you wanted to say. As if it might be dangerous, even. Listening to him talking about writing in the classroom or in the living room of the big Victorian house he shared with Tess Gallagher in Syracuse, you sensed a writer who loved the words of the masters who had handed the language down to him, and who was concerned that he might not be worthy to pick up the instrument. You feel this respect for the language—humility bordering on dread—in every sentence of his work.

Encountering Carver's fiction early in the seventies was a transforming experience for many writers of my generation, an experience perhaps comparable to discovering Hemingway's sentences in the twenties. In fact, Carver's language was unmistakably like Hemingway's—the simplicity and clarity, the repetitions, the nearly conversational rhythms, the precision of physical description. But Carver completely dispensed with the romantic egoism that made the Hemingway idiom such an awkward model for other writers in the late twentieth century. The cafés and pensions and battlefields of Europe were replaced by trailer parks and apartment complexes, the glamorous occupations by dead-end jobs. The trout in Carver's streams were apt to be pollution-deformed mutants. The good *vin du pays* was replaced by cheap gin, the romance of drinking by the dull grind of full-time alcoholism. Some commentators found his work depressing for these reasons. For many young writers, it was terribly liberating.

One aspect of what Carver seemed to say to us—even to someone who had never been inside a lumber mill or a trailer park—was that literature could be fashioned out of strict observation of real life, wherever and however it was lived, even if it was lived with a bottle of Heinz ketchup on the table and the television set droning. This was news at a time when academic metafiction was the regnant mode. His example reinvigorated realism as well as the short-story form.

Though he was a teacher for much of his life, Carver never

consciously gathered a band of disciples around himself. But when I was knocking around between graduate schools and the New York publishing world in the late seventies and early eighties, no other writer was as much discussed and mimicked by the writers one met at readings and writers' conferences. Probably not since Donald Barthelme began publishing in the sixties had a story writer generated such a buzz in the literary world.

Having fallen under Carver's spell on reading his first collection, *Will You Please Be Quiet, Please?*, a book I would have bought on the basis of the title alone, I was lucky enough to meet him a few years later and eventually to become his student at Syracuse University in the early eighties. Despite the existence of several thousand creative writing programs around the country, there is probably no good answer to the question of whether writing can be taught. Saying that Faulkner and Fitzgerald never got MFA's is beside the point. Novelists and short-story writers like to eat as much as anyone else, and tend to sniff out subsidies while they pursue their creative work. For writers in the twenties, the exchange rate was favorable in Paris, and in the thirties there was the WPA, and a gold rush of sorts in Hollywood. The universities have become the creative writers' WPA in recent years.

Carver was himself a product of the new system, having studied writing at the University of Iowa Writers' Workshop and at Stanford, and later earned a living teaching. It was something he did out of necessity, a role he was uncomfortable with. He did it to make a living, because it was easier than the other jobs he'd had—working at a sawmill and a hospital, working as a service station attendant, a janitor, a delivery boy, a textbook editor. Though grateful for genteel employment, he didn't really see why people who had a gift for writing should necessarily be able to teach. And he was very shy. The idea of facing a class made him nervous every time. On the days he had to teach he would get agitated, as if he himself were a student on the day of the final exam.

Like many writers in residence at universities, Ray was required to teach English courses in addition to creative writing courses. One was called Form and Theory of the Short Story, a title Ray inherited from the graduate English catalog. His method in these classes was to assign a book of stories he liked each week, including contemporary and nineteenth-century authors as well as works in translation. We would read the books and discuss them for two hours. Flannery O'Connor, Chekhov, Ann Beattie, Maupassant, Frank O'Connor, John Cheever, Mary Robison, Turgenev, and more Chekhov. (He loved all the nineteenth-century Russians.) Class would begin with Ray saying something like, "Well, guys, how'd you like Eudora Welty?" He preferred listening to lecturing, but he would read his favorite passages, talk about what he loved in the book he had chosen. He dealt in specifics, stayed close to the text, and eventually there would come a moment when the nervousness would lift off of him as he spoke about writing that moved him.

One semester, a very earnest Ph.D. candidate found his way into this class, composed mainly of writers. At that time, the English department, like many around the country, had become a battleground between theorists and humanists, and post-structuralism lay heavy upon the campus. After a few weeks of Carver's free-ranging and impressionistic approach to literature, the young theorist registered a strong protest: "This class is called Form and Theory of the Short Story but all we do is sit around and talk about the books. Where's the form and the theory?"

Ray looked distressed. He nodded and pulled extra hard on his cigarette. "Well, that's a good question," he said. After a long pause, he said, "I guess I'd say that the point here is that we read good books and discuss them.... And then you form your own theory." Then he smiled.

As a teacher of creative writing, too, Carver had a light touch. He did not consider it his job to discourage anyone. He said that there was enough discouragement out there for anyone trying against all odds to be a writer, and he clearly spoke from experience. Criticism, like fiction, was an act of empathy for Ray, putting yourself in the other guy's shoes. He couldn't understand writers who wrote negative reviews and once chided me for doing so. He believed fiction and poetry were fraternal enterprises. Among the very few people that Ray vocally disliked were a poet who had refused to lend him $50 when his car broke down in Salt Lake City; two critics who had attacked his own work, and writers who had attacked any of his friends.

For a shy man, his gregarious generosity of spirit was remarkable. He kept up a correspondence with dozens of other writers, students and fans. He wrote letters of recommendation and encouragement, helped people get jobs and grants, editors and agents, accompanied friends in need to their first AA meetings.

One day when I berated him for going easy on a student I thought was turning out poor work, he told me a story: he had recently been a judge in a prestigious fiction contest. The unanimous winner, whose work has since drawn much praise, turned out to be a former student of his, probably the worst, least promising student he'd had in twenty years. "What if I had discouraged her?" he said. His harshest critical formula was: "I think it's good you got that story behind you." Meaning, I guess, that one has to drive through some ugly country on the way to Parnassus. If Carver had had his way, classes and workshops would have been conducted entirely by students, but his approval was too highly valued for him to remain mute.

Once he sat through the reading of a long, strange story in his graduate writing workshop: as I recall, the story fleshed out two disparate characters, brought them together, followed their courtship and eventual marriage. After a series of false starts they decided to open a restaurant together, the preparations for which were described in great detail. On the day it opened a band of submachine-gun-toting terrorists burst in and killed everyone in the restaurant. End of story. After nearly everyone in the smoky seminar room had expressed dissatisfaction with this plot, we all turned to Ray. He was clearly at a loss. Finally he said softly, "Well, sometimes a story needs a submachine gun." This answer seemed to satisfy the author no less than those who felt the story in question had been efficiently put out of its misery.

My first semester, Ray somehow forgot to enter my grade for workshop. I pointed this out to him, and we went together to the English office to rectify the situation. "You did some real good work," he said, informing me that I would get an A. I was very pleased with myself, but perhaps a little less so when Ray opened the grade book and wrote an A next to my name underneath a solid column of identical grades. Everybody did good work, apparently. In workshop he approached every story with respect—treating each as if it were a living entity, a little sick, possibly, or lame, but something that could be nursed and trained to health.

Though Ray was always encouraging, he could be rigorous if he knew criticism was welcome. Fortunate students had their stories subjected to the same process he employed on his own numerous drafts. Manuscripts came back thoroughly ventilated with Carver deletions, substitutions, question marks, and chicken-scratch queries. I took one story back to him seven times; he must have spent fifteen or twenty hours on it. He was a meticulous, obsessive line editor. One on one, in his office, he almost became a tough guy, his voice gradually swelling with conviction.

Once we spent some ten or fifteen minutes debating my use of the word "earth." Carver felt it had to be "ground," and he felt it was worth the trouble of talking it through. That one exchange was invaluable; I think of it constantly when I'm working. Carver himself used the same example later in an essay he wrote that year, in discussing the influence of his mentor, John Gardner. "Ground is ground, he'd say, it means ground, dirt, that kind of stuff. But if you say 'earth,' that's something else, that word has other ramifications."

John Gardner, the novelist, was Ray's first writing teacher. They met at Chico State College in California in the sixties. Ray said that all of his writing life he had felt Gardner looking over his shoulder when he wrote, approving or disapproving of certain words, phrases, and strategies. Calling fouls. He said a good writing teacher is something like a literary conscience, a friendly critical voice in your ear. I know what he meant. (I have one; it mumbles.) After almost twenty years Carver had a reunion with his old teacher, who was living and teaching less than a hundred miles from Syracuse, in Binghamton, New York, and Gardner's approval of his work had meant a great deal to him. In the spring of 1982, I happened to stop by Ray's house a few minutes after he heard that Gardner had died in a motorcycle crash. Distraught, he couldn't sit still. We walked around the house and the backyard as he talked about Gardner.

"Back then I didn't even know what a writer looked like," Ray said. "John looked like a writer. He had that hair, and he used to wear this thing that was like a cape. I tried to copy the way he walked. He used to let me work in his office because I didn't have a quiet place to work. I'd go through his files and steal the titles of his stories, use them on my stories."

So he must have understood when we all shamelessly cribbed from him, we students at Syracuse and Iowa and Stanford and all the other writing workshops in the country where almost everyone seemed to be writing and publishing stories with Raymond Carver titles like "Do You Mind if I Smoke?" or "How About This, Honey?" He certainly didn't want clones. But he knew that imitation was part of finding your own voice.

I encountered Carver near the beginning of what he liked to call his "second life," after he had quit drinking. I heard stories about the bad old Ray, stories he liked to tell on himself. When I met him, I thought of writers as luminous madmen who drank too much and drove too fast and scattered brilliant pages along their doomed trajectories. Maybe at one time he did, too. In his essay "Fires," he says, "I understood writers to be people who didn't spend their Saturdays at the Laundromat." Would Hemingway be caught dead doing laundry? No, but William Carlos Williams would. Ditto Carver's beloved Chekhov. In the classroom and on the page, Carver somehow delivered the tonic news that there was laundry in the kingdom of letters.

Not that, by this time, Ray was spending much time at the Laundromat, life having been good to him toward the end in a way for which he seemed constantly to be grateful. But hearing the typewriter of one of the masters of American prose clacking just up the street, while a neighbor raked leaves and some kids threw a Frisbee as the dogs went on with their doggy life—this was a lesson in itself for me. Whatever dark mysteries lurk at the heart of the writing process, he insisted on a single trade secret: that you had to survive, find some quiet, and work hard every day. And seeing him for coffee, or watching a ball game or a dumb movie with him, put into perspective certain dangerous myths about the writing life that he preferred not to lecture on—although he sometimes would, if he thought it might help. When we first became acquainted, in New York, he felt obliged to advise me, in a series of wonderful letters, and a year later I moved upstate to become his student.

Reading the dialogues of Plato, one eventually realizes that Socrates' self-deprecation is something of a ploy. Ray's humility, however, was profound and unself-conscious and one of the most astonishing things about him. When he asked a student, "What do you think?" he clearly wanted to know. This seemed a rare and inspiring didactic stance. His own opinions were expressed with such caution that you knew how carefully they had been measured.

For someone who claimed he didn't love to teach, he made a great deal of difference to a great many students. He certainly changed my life irrevocably, and I have heard others say the same thing.

I'm still leaning forward with my head cocked to one side, straining to hear his voice.

Getting in Touch with Your Child
from *Story of My Life*

I'M LIKE, I DON'T believe this shit.

I'm totally pissed at my old man who's somewhere in the Virgin Islands, I don't know where. The check wasn't in the mailbox today which means I can't go to school Monday morning. I'm on the monthly payment program because Dad says wanting to be an actress is some flaky whim and I never stick to anything—this from a guy who's been married five times—and this way if I drop out in the middle of the semester he won't get burned for the full tuition. Meanwhile he buys his new bimbo Tanya who's a year younger than me a 450 SL convertible—always gone for the young ones, haven't we, Dad?—plus her own condo so she can have some privacy to do her writing. Like she can even *read*. He actually believes her when she says she's writing a novel but when I want to spend eight hours a day busting ass at Lee Strasberg it's like, *another one of Alison's crazy ideas.* Story of my life. My old man is fifty-two going on twelve. And then there's Skip Pendleton, which is another reason I'm pissed.

So I'm on the phone screaming at my father's secretary when there's a call on my other line. I go hello and this guy goes, hi, I'm whatever-his-name-is, I'm a friend of Skip's and I say yeah? and he says, I thought maybe we could go out sometime.

And I say, what am I, dial-a-date?

Skip Pendleton's this jerk I was in lust with once for about three minutes. He hasn't called me in like three weeks which is fine, okay, I can deal with that, but suddenly I'm like a baseball card he trades with his friends? Give me a break. So I go to this guy, what makes you think I'd want to go out with you, I don't even know you? and he says, Skip told me about you. Right. So I'm like, what did he tell you? and the guy goes—Skip said you were hot. I say, great, I'm totally honored that the great Skip Pendleton thinks I'm hot. I'm just a jalapeño pepper waiting for some strange burrito, honey. I mean, *really*.

And this guy says to me, we were sitting around at Skip's place about five in the morning the other night wired out of our minds and I say—this is the guy talking—I wish we had some women and Skip is like, I could always call Alison, she'd be over like a shot.

He said that? I say. I can hear his voice exactly, it's not like I'm totally amazed, but still I can't believe even he would be such a pig and suddenly I feel like a cheap slut and I want to scream at this asshole but instead I say, where are you? He's on West Eighty-ninth, it figures, so I give him an address on Avenue C, a rathole where a friend of mine lived last year until her place was broken into for the seventeenth time and which is about as far away from the Upper West Side as you can get without crossing water, so I tell him to meet me there in an hour and at least I have the satisfaction of thinking of him spending about twenty bucks for a cab and then hanging around the doorway of this tenement and maybe getting beat up by some drug dealers. But the one I'm really pissed at is Skip Pendleton. Nothing my father does surprises me anymore. I'm twenty going on gray.

Skip is thirty-one and he's so smart and so educated—just ask him, he'll tell you. A legend in his own mind. Did I forget to mention he's *so* mature? Unlike me. He was always telling me I don't know anything. I'll tell you one thing I don't know—I don't know what I saw in him. He seemed older and sophisticated and we had great sex, so why not? I met him in a club, naturally. I never thought he was very good-looking, but you could tell he thought he was. He believed it so much he could actually sell other people on the idea. He has that confidence everybody wants a piece of. This blond hair that looks like he has it trimmed about three times a day. Nice clothes, shirts custom-made on Jermyn Street, which he might just casually tell you some night in case you didn't know is in London, England. (That's in Europe, which is across the Atlantic Ocean—oh, really Skip, is that where it is? Wow!) Went to the right schools. And he's rich, of course, owns his own company. Commodities trader. Story of Skip's life, trading commodities.

So basically, he has it all. Should be a Dewar's Profile, I'm like amazed they haven't asked him yet. But when the sun hit him in the morning he was a shivering wreck.

From the first night, bending over the silver picture frame in his apartment with a rolled fifty up his nose, all he can talk about is his ex, and how if he could only get her back he'd give up all of this forever—coke, staying out partying all night, young bimbos like me. And I'm thinking, poor guy just lost his main squeeze, feeling real sympathetic and so like I go, when did this happen, Skip? and it turns out it was ten years ago! He lived with this chick for four years at Harvard and then after they come to New York together she dumps him. And I'm like, give me a break, Skip. Give yourself a break. This is ten years after. This is nineteen eighty-whatever.

Skip's so smart, right? My parents never gave a shit whether I went to school or not, they were off chasing lovers and bottles, leaving us kids with the cars and the credit cards, and I never did get much of an education. Is that my fault? I mean, if someone told you back then that you could either go to school or not, what do you think you would have done? Pass the trigonometry, please. Right. So I'm not as educated as the great Skip Pendleton, but let me tell you—I know that when you're hitting on someone you don't spend the whole night whining about your ex, especially after like a decade. And you don't need a Ph.D. in psychology to figure out why Skip can't go out with anybody his own age. He keeps trying to find Diana, the beautiful, perfect Diana who was twenty-one when she said sayonara. And he wants us, the young stuff, because we're like Diana was in the good old days. And he hates us because we're not Diana. And he thinks it will make him feel better if he fucks us over and makes us hurt the way he was hurt, because that's what it's all about if you ask me—we're all sitting around here on earth working through our hurts, trying to pass them along to other people and make things even. Chain of pain.

Old Skip kept telling me how dumb I was. You wish, Jack. Funny thing is, dumb is his type. He doesn't want to go out with anybody who might see through him, so he picks up girls like me. Girls he thinks will believe everything he says and fuck him the first night and not be real surprised when he never calls again.

If you're so smart, Skip, how come you don't know these things? If you're so mature, what were you doing with me?

Men. I've never met any. They're all boys. I wish I didn't want them so much. I've had a few dreams about making it with girls, but it's kind of like—sure, I'd love to visit Norway sometime. My roommate Jeannie and I sleep in the same bed and it's great. We've got a one-bedroom and this way the living room is free for partying and whatever. I hate being alone, but when I wake up in some guy's bed with dry come on the sheets and he's snoring like a garbage truck, I go—let me out of here. I slip out and crawl around the floor groping for my clothes, trying to untangle his blue jeans from mine, my bra from his Jockeys—Skip wears boxers, of course—without making any noise, out the door and home to where Jeannie has been warming the bed all night. Jumping in between the sheets and she wakes up and goes, I want details, Alison—length and width.

I love Jeannie. She cracks me up. She's an assistant editor at a fashion magazine but what she really wants to do is get married. It might work for her but I don't believe in it. My parents have seven marriages between them and any time I've been with a guy for more than a few weeks I find myself looking out the window during sex.

Jay McInerney ⟫⟫⟫⟪⟪⟪ 27

I CALL UP MY FRIEND DIDI to see if she can lend me the money. Didi's father's rich and he gives her this huge allowance, but she spends it all on blow. She used to buy clothes but now she wears the same outfit for four or five days in a row and it's pretty gross, let me tell you. Sometimes we have to send the health department over to her apartment to open the windows and burn the sheets.

I get Didi's machine, which means she's not home. If she's home she unplugs the phone and if she's not home she turns on the answering machine. Either way it's pretty impossible to get hold of her. She sleeps from about noon till like 9:00 P.M. or so. If Didi made a list of her favorite things I guess cocaine would be at the top and sunlight wouldn't even make the cut.

My friends and I spend half our lives leaving messages for each other. Luckily I know Didi's message access code so I dial again and listen to her messages to see if I can figure out from the messages where she is. Okay, maybe I'm just nosy.

The first message is from Wick and from his voice I can tell that he's doing Didi, which really blows me away, since Wick is Jeannie's old boyfriend. Except that Didi is less interested in sex than anybody I know so I'm not really sure. Maybe Wick is just starting to make his move. A message from her mom—call me, sweetie, I'm in Aspen. Then Emile, saying he wants his three hundred and fifty dollars or else. Which is when I go—what am I, crazy? I'm never going to get a cent out of Didi. If I even try she'll talk me into getting wired with her and I'm trying to stay away from that. I'm about to hang up when I get a call on the other line. It's my school telling me that my tuition hasn't arrived and that I can't come back to class until it does. Like, what do you think I've been frantic about for the last twenty-four hours? It's Saturday afternoon. Jeannie will be home soon and then it's all over.

By this time I'm getting pretty bitter. You could say I am not a happy unit. Acting is the first thing I've ever really wanted to do.

Except for riding. When I was a kid I spent most of my time on horseback. I went around the country, showing my horses and jumping, until Dangerous Dan dropped dead. I loved Dan more than just about any living thing since and that was it for me and horses. That's what happens, basically, when you love something. It's like, you can't get rid of the shit you don't like, I have this rotten crinoline dress that's been following me from apartment to apartment for years, but every time I find something I really love one of my sisters or girl-friends disappears with it the next day. Actually, we all trade clothes, hardly anybody I know would think of leaving the house without wearing something borrowed or stolen, if it was just clothes I'd be like, no problem, but that's another story.

So anyway, after horses I got into drugs. But acting, I don't know, I just love it, getting up there and turning myself inside out. Being somebody else for a change. It's like being a child again, playing at something, making believe, laughing and crying all over the place, ever since I can remember people have been trying to get me to stifle my emotions but forget it—I'm an emotional kind of girl. My drama teacher has this great thing he always says—get in touch with your child, which is supposed to be the raw, uncensored part of yourself. Acting is about being true to your feelings, which is great since real life seems to be about being a liar and a hypocrite.

Acting is the first thing that's made me get up in the morning. The first year I was in New York I didn't do anything but guys and blow. Staying out all night at the Surf Club and Zulu, waking up at five in the afternoon with plugged sinuses and sticky hair. Some kind of white stuff in every opening. Story of my life. My friends are still pretty much that way which is why I'm so desperate to get this check because if I don't then there's no reason to wake up early Monday morning and Jeannie will get home and somebody will call up and the next thing I know it'll be three days from now with no sleep in between, brain in orbit, nose in traction. I call my father's secretary again and she says she's still trying to reach him.

I decide to do some of my homework before Jeannie gets home—my sense-memory exercise. Don't ask me why, since I won't be able to go to school. But it chills me out. I sit down in the folding chair and relax, empty my mind of all the crap. Then I begin to imagine an orange. I try to see it in front of me. I take it in my hand. A big old round one veined with rust, like the ones you get down in Florida straight from the tree. (Those Clearasil spotless ones you buy in the Safeway are dusted with cyanide or some such shit so you can imagine how good they are for you.) So I start to peel it real slow, smelling the little geysers of spray that break from the squeezed peel, feeling the juice stinging around the edges of my fingernails where I've bitten them....

So of course the phone rings. A guy's voice, Barry something, says, may I please speak to Alison Poole?

And I'm like, you're doing it.

I'm a friend of Skip's, he says.

I go, if this is some kind of joke I'm like really not amused.

Hey, no joke, he goes. I'm just, you know, Skip told me you guys weren't going out anymore and I saw you once at Indochine and I thought maybe we could do dinner sometime.

I'm like, I don't believe this. What am I?—the York Avenue Escort Service?

I go, did Skip also tell you about the disease he gave me? That shrinks this Barry's equipment pretty quick. Suddenly he's got a call on his other line. Sure you do.

It's true—that was Skip's little going-away present. Morning after the last night I slept with him I was really sore and itchy and then I get this weird rash so I finally go to the doctor who gives me this big lecture on AIDS—yada yada yada—then says the rash is a sexually transmitted thing that won't kill me but I have to take these antibiotics for two weeks and not sleep with anybody in the meantime. I go, two weeks, who do you think I am, the Virgin Mary? and she goes, as your doctor I think I know your habits well enough to know what a sacrifice this will be for you, Alison. Then she gives me the usual about why don't I make them wear condoms and I'm like, for the same reason I don't fuck with my clothes on, you can't beat flesh on flesh. I want contact, right? Just give me direct contact and you can keep true love.

Anyway I never did tell Skip, I don't know why, I guess I just didn't want to talk to him, the son of a bitch.

So I'm smoking a cigarette, thumbing through my *Actors' Scenebook*, sort of looking for a monologue, I've got to get one for next week but I haven't found anything I like, I start browsing around the other sections, Monologues for Men, Scenes for Two Women—no thanks—Scenes for One Man and One Woman. Which is about the worst scene there is.

The phone rings again and it's Didi. Unbelievable! Live-in person, practically. And it's daylight outside.

I just went to my nose doctor, she goes. He was horrified. Told me that if I had to keep doing blow I should start shooting up, then the damage would be some other doctor's responsibility.

What's with you and Wick? I say.

I don't know, she goes, I went home with him a couple of weeks ago. I woke up in his bed. I'm not even sure we did anything. But he's definitely in lust with me. Meanwhile, my period's late. So maybe we did.

Didi has another call. While she takes it, I'm thinking. The wheels are turning—wheels within wheels. Didi comes back on and tells me it's her mom, who's having a major breakdown, she'll call me back. I tell her no problem. She's already been a big help.

I GET SKIP AT HIS OFFICE. He doesn't sound too thrilled to hear from me. He says he's in a meeting, can he call me back?

I say no, I have to talk now.

What's up? he says.

I go, I'm pregnant.

Total silence.

Before he can ask I tell him I haven't slept with anybody else in six weeks. Which is totally true, almost. Close off that little escape hatch in his mind. Wham, bam, thank you ma'am.

He goes, you're sure? He sounds like he's just swallowed a bunch of sand.

I'm sure, I say.

He's like, what do you want to do?

The thing about Skip is that even though he's an asshole, he's also a gentleman. Actually a lot of the assholes I know are gentlemen. Or vice versa. Dickheads with a family crest and a prep-school code of honor.

When I say I need money he asks how much.

A thousand, I say. I can't believe I ask him for that much, I was thinking five hundred just a minute ago, but hearing his voice pisses me off.

He asks if I want him to go with me and I say no, definitely not. Then he tries to do this number about making out the check directly to the clinic and I say, Skip, don't give me that shit. I need five hundred in cash to make the appointment, I tell him, and I don't want to wait six business days for the stupid check to clear, okay? Acting my ass off. My teacher would be proud.

Two hours later a messenger arrives with the money. Cash. I give him a ten-dollar tip.

SATURDAY NIGHT JEANNIE AND DIDI go out. Didi comes over, wearing this same horrible surfer shirt she's had on all week and her blond rastafarian hair. Really gross. But she's still incredibly beautiful, even four days without sleep, and guys make total asses of themselves trying to pick her up. Her mother was this really big model in the fifties, Swedish. Didi was supposed to be the Revlon Girl or something but she couldn't be bothered to wake up for the shoot.

Jeannie's wearing my black cashmere sweater, a couple yards of pearls, jeans and Maude Frizon pumps.

How do I look? she goes, checking herself out in the mirror.

Terrific, I say. You'll be lucky if you make it through cocktails without getting raped.

Can't rape the willing, Jeannie says, which is what we always say.

They try to get me to come along, but I'm doing my scene for class Monday morning. They can't believe it. They say it won't last. I go, this is my life. I'm like trying to do something constructive with it, you know? Jeannie and Didi think this is hilarious. They do this choirgirl thing where they both fold their hands like they're praying and hum "Amazing Grace," which is what we do when somebody starts to get religious on us. Then, just to be complete assholes, they sing, *Alison, we know this world is killing you...* et cetera, which is kind of like my theme song when I'm being a drag.

So I go:

> *They say you're nothing but party girls*
> *Just like a million more all over the world*

They crack up. We all love Costello.

After they finally leave, I open up my script but I'm having trouble concentrating, it's this play called *Mourning Becomes Electra*, so I call up my little sister at home. Of course the line is busy and they don't have call waiting so I call the operator and request an emergency breakthrough on the line. I listen while the operator cuts in. I hear Carol's voice and then the operator says there's an emergency call from Vanna White in New York. Carol immediately says Alison, in this moaning, grown-up voice even though she's three years younger than me.

What's new? I go when she gets rid of the other call.

Same old stuff, she says. Mom's drunk. My car's in the shop. Mickey's out on bail. He's drunk, too.

Listen, do you know where Dad is? I go and she says, Virgin Islands last she heard, maybe St. Croix but she doesn't have a number either. So I tell her about my school thing and then maybe because I'm feeling a little weird about it I tell her about Skip, except I say five hundred dollars instead of a thousand, and she says it sounds like he totally deserved it. He's such a prick, I go, and Carol says, yeah, he sounds just like Dad.

And I go, yeah, just like.

JEANNIE COMES BACK Sunday morning at 9:00 A.M. She's a shivering wreck. For a change I'm just waking up instead of just going to sleep. I give Jeannie a Valium and put her to bed. It's sort of a righteous feeling, being on this end of the whole experience—I feel like a doctor or something.

She lies in bed stiff as a mannequin and says, I'm so afraid, Alison. She is not a happy unit.

We're all afraid, I go.

In half an hour she's making these horrible chainsaw sleep noises.

THANKS TO SKIP, Monday morning I'm at school doing dance and voice. Paid my bill in cash. Now I'm feeling great. Real good. In the afternoon I've got acting class. We start with sense-memory work. I sit down in class and my teacher tells me I'm at a beach. He wants me to see the sand and the water and feel the sun on my bare skin. Hear the volleyballs whizzing past. No problem. First I have to clear myself out. That's part of the process. All around me people are making strange noises, stretching, getting their yayas out, preparing for their own exercises. Some people I swear, even though this is supposed to be totally spontaneous, you can always tell some of these people are acting for the teacher even in warm-up, laughing or crying so dramatically, like, *look at me, I'm so spontaneous.* There's a lot of phonies in this profession. Anyway, I don't know—I'm just letting myself go limp in the head, then I'm laughing hysterically and next thing I'm bawling like a baby, really out of control, falling out of my chair and thrashing all over the floor...a real basket case...epileptic apocalypse, sobbing and flailing around, trying to take a bite out of the linoleum...they're used to some pretty radical emoting in here, but this is way over the top, apparently. I kind of lose it, and the nurse says I'm overtired and tells me to go home and rest....

THAT NIGHT MY OLD MAN finally calls. I'm like, I must be dreaming.

Pissed at you, I go, when he asks how I am.

I'm sorry, honey, he says, about the tuition. I screwed up.

You're goddamn right you did, I say.

Oh, baby, he goes, I'm a mess.

You're telling me, I go.

He says, she left me.

Don't come crying to me about what's-her-name, I say. Then he starts to whine and I go, when are you going to grow up, for Christ's sake?

I bitch him out for a while and then I tell him I'm sorry, it's okay, he's well rid of her, there's lots of women who would love a sweet man like him. Not to mention his money. Story of his life. But I don't say that of course. He's fifty-two years old and it's a little late to teach him the facts of life. From what I've seen nobody changes much after a certain age. Like about four years old, maybe. Anyway, I hold his hand and cool him out and almost forget to hit him up for money.

Jay McInerney »»»««« 35

He promises to send me the tuition and the rent and something extra. I'm not holding my breath.

I should hate my father, sometimes I think I do. There was a girl in the news the last few weeks, she hired her boyfriend to shoot her old man. Families, Jesus. At least with lovers you can break up. These old novels and plays that always start out with orphans, in the end they find their parents—I want to say, don't look for them, you're better off without. Believe me. Get a dog instead. That's one of my big ambitions in life—to be an orphan. With a trust fund, of course. And a harem of men to come and go as I command, guys as beautiful and faceless as the men who lay you down in your dreams.

Tess Gallagher

TESS GALLAGHER is a poet, short story writer, and essayist. Her most recent books include *Soul Barnacles* (essays, University of Michigan, 2000), *At the Owl Woman Saloon* (stories, Simon & Schuster, 1999); *Portable Kisses* (poems, Bloodaxe, 1996), and *My Black Horse: New and Selected Poems* (Bloodaxe, 1995). Ms. Gallagher handles all matters concerning the work of her late husband, Raymond Carver.

Two Mentors:
From Orphanhood to
Spirit-Companion

>>>>>>>>>>>>>>>>>>>>>>>X<<<<<<<<<<<<<<<<<<<<

I was orphaned at the gate, really. My first mentor, Theodore Roethke, crossed into posterity so soon after our meeting that I doubt he realized or, if he had, would have accepted his status as mentor to me. Years after, I had the luck to find another witnessing and abiding presence in Stanley Kunitz. He has sojourned with me for nearly twenty-five years, attentive when I have approached and always *with* me in some unquantifiable way that supports this endeavor, this life of becoming and remaining a poet.

As to Roethke, I cherish him deeply, and, through him, during the invitation and eventual sustenance of his last class at the University of Washington in spring of 1963, I met my strongest sense of what poetry might be. I was eighteen and had just taken my baby steps as a poet. Roethke managed to instill a sense of rigor and music and mystery that would guide me to the present moment. His stress on memorization as a way to take in a poem's body physically and psychically at the cellular level and thereby pass its elements into one's deep consciousness has remained primary in my way of teaching myself and my students for nearly thirty years. It's still the best way to train the ear to absorb the intricate sonic and rhythmic turns of a poem. From Roethke I took up and carried the work of poets who are with me to this day as models and inspiration—Louise Bogan and W. B. Yeats chief among them.

Roethke's erratic bodily movements and gestures in the classroom could be downright scary as he careened or rocked out a poem's rhythms. He had a distracted presence that, like a telephoto lens, was nonetheless liable to snap into close-up. More than once I found myself in the clearing with his attention focused intently on me. I never felt worthy, but he took note of me anyway. Those times I recited a poem, or read aloud from the work of the poets he'd assigned, or when he spoke of my poems, served as an initiation of sorts. When dealing with our poems, he would focus on a phrase or line to admire, to savor, and by such threads I survived. I wouldn't say he was kindly, but rather more like one looking ahead into a distance at the writers we might become, if he could give us a foothold. And he did give that, for me and others in that class.

Still, I clawed fingerholds into granite to feel I belonged in that company. I was a logger's daughter. I hadn't read or even written much. Whatever he said to do, try, or read—I did. There has been a peculiar echo effect from some of the notions I picked up in his class. Years later, things he said would make sense. I met Roethke during his metaphysical stage, and this would make me unfit for the sort of poetry which is daily, chatty, and which doesn't rely heavily on the consequentiality of its subject matter. I knew there were legitimately many kinds of poems to which one might aspire, but Roethke let me see that angels could indeed stand on our shoulders, as in Rilke, and that we had to be ready to carry the cargo we might discover in the presence of powers beyond our own. That's where rigor came in—reading and trying to write as well as one could in preparation for the strenuousness of the journey. None of this was spelled out, yet I know that Roethke gave us a sense of what to hope for as the intensity of one's experience entered language, often in ways quite beyond us.

Roethke never knew he was my mentor, for our time together passed in three short months. This was probably fortunate, for I eventually read letters in his archives in which he gently rebuffed attempts by others, such as James Wright, to draw him into the sphere of their writerly struggles. Roethke died of a heart attack in a swimming pool that summer following our class, and when it happened I felt a great unfairness had befallen me. He had quickened desire for the craft and endeavor of a life in poetry, but was not there to nurture it. I recall the moment I learned of his death, my hands in dishwater where I worked bussing tables at a hometown restaurant to earn money in order to return to college that fall. The radio on the shelf above the sink gave the news as innocently as weather, and the tears I shed fell stupidly, helplessly into the dishwater. The cook, a woman with gold crosses in her ears who pilfered the till, was, all in all, a good old sort. She tried to comfort me and told the owner of the restaurant that *a family member* had passed away so I'd be let off the rest of the evening. Indeed, this was not far from the truth, for losing Roethke was like losing a father.

Perhaps the full magic of finding an ongoing mentor only struck me when I connected with Stanley Kunitz through the mails in 1972 and finally met him in 1976. I had been carried by Roethke for the thirteen intervening years of my orphanhood, and by my strong desire to be a poet, certified, I felt, by Roethke's having entered my life, and then by my own spiritual ability to survive on what he'd given me.

Kunitz made me feel fathered again in my art. Although he never *worked* on or assessed my poems in manuscript, as I know he did with others he mentored more formally, he recognized me and continued to hold faith in me during periods when my work needed to grow in other directions, as when I took time to write stories, or work in film with Robert Altman, or as of late, when I've been absorbed with tending Raymond Carver's work.

Our friendship developed from my discovery of Akhmatova in Kunitz's translations of her in 1975 while I was an MFA student at the University of Iowa Writers' workshop. Subsequently he chose poems of mine to present in *American Poetry Review*. Thereafter, we would meet usually once a year in New York City or on the rare times I went to Provincetown, Massachusetts, where he spent the summer.

Years later, in 1997, at ninety-three, Stanley crossed America with one small bag and met me in the Seattle airport to travel with me to Walla Walla and Whitman College where I had taught as the Edward F. Arnold Chair in 1996–97. Our trip together was a precious gift to me. While there, Stanley gave a splendid class to undergraduates as the first reader for the Walt Whitman Reading Series, and he met some of my former students. We would have our own quiet talks en route or prior to events. He had followed my life and loves, had seen one marriage end and then the happy advent of Raymond Carver in my life. After Ray's death, he'd become, if possible, even more important.

Because the poems I'd written in *Moon Crossing Bridge* had lifted and sustained me, despite the seriousness of their cargo, I admit I was caught by surprise when Stanley told me he'd had a hard time reading them. He confessed to having been so personally concerned for me that he couldn't really take in the poems. I was mindful of his own father's suicide prior to his birth and understood its haunting power. It was a very human and tender admission—for him to have feared for me, as a result of the poems.

Nonetheless, he had mistaken the affect of the poems on me. Far from leading me to any break with life, they had in fact delivered me back to the shore on which I had gained full strength, having withstood the fire of those poems long enough to forge a way to carry meaningfully the experience of losing my soulmate and deep love, Raymond Carver, who had died of lung cancer at age fifty. I was inescapably disappointed that what I felt to be my best writing so far had not been received by my mentor in the way I'd hoped.

Yet even this would be a step in my growth. It let me see that I had passed beyond that portal where one wishes simply to achieve a hoped-for *well done*. I grew by seeing that I had needed to write those poems so urgently that I was willing for the entire world to shut its mind and soul to me. If I'd written in anticipation of reception, I might have been deeply wounded by Stanley's apprehension—his sense, finally, that I had crossed too far over into the zone of the dead to bring back those poems. But I had not known what to expect from any quarter, and Stanley's reaction seemed actually to free me. I returned to prose, my next inclination, since prose, of necessity, frees one from the ego and takes one back more openly to the world of others.

Our time together at Whitman College put Stanley and me on our best intuitive ground with each other—that place where one feels a deep joy at being perfectly received, valued, respected in one's entire being. Unlike with Roethke, Stanley's mentorship of me was accepted and acknowledged. He knew I looked to him for that currency the world at large can't really give, but which must be given by one far-seeing, attentive soul-consciousness to another. Just being with Stanley reminded me of the wisdom I'd learned from a man with whom I'd caught a lift on the roads near Sligo once in my youth: *Go and say nothing,* he'd told me when I confided that I was on the way to straighten out a misunderstanding with a friend. So it was with Stanley. We didn't revisit any site of the past, but simply and purely enjoyed each other's company. At one telling moment, however, he turned and said quietly, *I'm not worried about you,* and I took it as a blessing.

The substance of what one receives from a mentor is hard to quantify or define. Let me say it this way: Stanley allowed me access to his own long engagement with several world literatures, with musical, incantational speech, with the wide sweep of his consciousness and intuitional insight as he took in, appraised, and caressed the world in language and acts.

An incident in Stanley's garden on the cape in Provincetown

comes back to me as an emblem of the affection and mystery of our relationship. I asked him if I might see the snake he'd told me lived there. Stanley looked down into the dense ground cover at our feet and seemed to know exactly where to reach. He didn't grasp; he simply offered his wrist and the garter snake twined around and along his forearm, flicking its tongue, and seemed perfectly at ease there, as if Stanley's arm were the branch of a familiar tree. *Go ahead, you can touch him,* Stanley said, running his free hand over the snake's back. I followed his example, and the snake seemed to accept the gesture, or at least to tolerate my stroking. Then Stanley bent and let the snake swirl down and away into the ground cover again.

This encounter would have taken no more than three minutes, but it has somehow codified the sharing of the mystery and deep entrustment mentoring can be. One doesn't know how it works. It just does. As with any relationship, there are hazards and turns—times one may panic and feel a bit lost or misapprehended. But the rediscovery and renegotiation of respect on a new level adds dimension and muscle to the companioning. Being mentored has been a spiritual enterprise from the start, because of my having lost Roethke so early. This development of ritual, of unseen and intuitive elements, thus became, for me, the most forceful reaching I could manage, and this strengthened my poetry and my life.

There is something of a fatedness to being mentored. For this reason, to thank a mentor might indicate that choice, on either part, has played a larger role than it has. Nonetheless, my heart is glad for these sustaining spirits, Roethke and Kunitz—grateful that fortune smiled early and long on me, to send me these very ones.

Behave

Central word of my childhood.
A father's plea that could turn
command, then verge on threat: *behave,*
I want you to behave now.
This bright morning promises a cathedral
when a chapel will do to praise this word, tender
enough over years to slice the distance
into the two halves of any question—
what we might have done and what we came
to do. To question such authority meant
a pirouette of backward glances or intention

like a freight train finding and loading up
its reasons. *If you don't behave,* he'd say,
desperation mounting for the din of household
to let him have, after the day's labor, some
riverbank-moment where stillness
could come, could eddy and release him back
into his "far away"—that place we could sense
him wanting to get to
like a drowning man whose life seems the far shore
when it is a breath at the lip
of a watery precipice

under him. Roethke, my other long gone father,
paraphrasing Marianne Moore
to tell us: *"Once we feel deeply*
we begin to behave."

The notion there of right action proceeding
naturally out of right feeling—
poetry the witching stick, not only to what was felt,
but how the ability to feel a thing
meant something already done to the good.

Standing near his grave in Saginaw,
after thirty-seven years of learning to behave
as empathy, art's slow-eyed handmaiden: wearing
in the bone the strictness and necessary solitude,
the passion of that mandate as it insists
on the instructing presence, especially of the dead—I do
behave, in my own way.
Roethke's great love of poetry seems to rise up
in welcome. I would tell him that for the spiritual child
there *are* rights in the matter, and also
that the child-heart of those first ungainly poems
he more than read, still strives in the ongoing restoration
a life in poetry can be. I squandered myself

these years to good purpose: to earn more
than a daughterly right, for which the language
was not always a friend. But the remaking of it
gradually, as poems teach, does enfold and lead us
to tenderness, despite the steely hammer blows that fall
as if the life too were steel,
when it is only that child in a doorway, that father
at the table with his head in his hands,
and the word *behave* finding me so audibly
I bend to the grave in fractured, wayward obedience

as one who is grateful, that like you, my fathers,
I knew to take a breath from the carnation
before giving it to stone.

Peter Taylor

David Huddle

DAVID HUDDLE's books include *Paper Boy, Stopping by Home, The High Spirits, Only the Little Bone, The Nature of Yearning, The Writing Habit, Intimates, A David Huddle Reader, Tenorman,* and *Summer Lake: New and Selected Poems.* Since 1971, Huddle has taught literature and creative writing at the University of Vermont. In 1999, Houghton Mifflin published his first novel, *The Story of a Million Years,* which was named a Distinguished Book of the year by *Esquire* and a Best Book of the year by the *Los Angeles Times.*

What About Those Good People?

>>>>>>>>>>>>>>>>>>>>>>>>><<<<<<<<<<<<<<<<<<<<

"I wonder when David's going to get around to writing about the good people of Southwest Virginia." These words of Peter Taylor's came to me a few years after his death. In the fall of 1996, I was in Charlottesville for a reading; the person introducing me was Peter's young fiction-writing confidante Mariflo Stephens, who happens to be the younger sister of my high school girlfriend, the late Melva Stephens. So in her introduction, Mariflo quoted this offhand remark that Peter had made in a conversation with her. It sounded so exactly like something he'd say about me that as I sat in my hard-bottomed folding chair, waiting to step up to the podium, I felt a little shiver, as if Peter had spoken directly to me from the other side of death. I knew what he meant. The comment had a history.

In September 1967 I requested permission to enroll in a graduate fiction-writing workshop at the University of Virginia. To discuss the matter, Peter Taylor and I met in his office in a house on Jefferson Park Avenue across from Cabell Hall. Mr. Taylor had just been hired to teach at U.Va., after many years on the faculty of the University of North Carolina at Greensboro. It was my first regular semester back at U.Va. after flunking out in 1964 and serving a hitch in the U.S. Army, the last ten months of it in Vietnam. So he and I came to that dark and cramped upstairs office from opposite sides of the planet. Formerly the

Women's College of North Carolina, UNC-Greensboro was a pretty decorous place. Though I hadn't experienced heavy combat, my months in Vietnam had nevertheless acquainted me with—as Esmé puts it in her famous story—"squalor." So what we had that day was a barbaric student requesting permission to study with an immensely refined teacher.

Mr. Taylor let me into his workshop that semester and the next, and as the school year went on, I became aware of his taking a teacher's friendly interest in me. He called on me to stay at his house to keep his teenage son company when he and Mrs. Taylor had to travel out of town. And he invited me to social occasions there, most memorably to a dinner party honoring James Dickey about a year before *Deliverance* came out. Mr. Taylor gently encouraged me to call him by his first name, and I gave it a try, but I never managed it with much grace. My upbringing—and even my army training—seemed to require me to call him Mister. He himself was an extremely mannerly person.

On the other hand, the fiction I wrote and handed in was almost belligerently crude. Maybe I felt a need to shock my gentlemanly teacher. More likely, though, squalor was just the place where I was in my literary evolution—somewhere around the Cro-Magnon phase. I remember one story in particular that graphically described a couple having sex on a kitchen table just before the big shotgun murder scene at the end. Mr. Taylor and I discussed that one in his office because he said he didn't feel that it was appropriate for workshop discussion. He said that he personally had no difficulties with writing about sex—he'd even done a bit of it himself—but that he didn't think that the members of the workshop who wouldn't feel comfortable with it should be forced to read and discuss such material. Though I was big on sex and violence in those days and hadn't begun to learn the meaning of the word *restraint*, Mr. Taylor didn't try in any overt way to civilize me. I'm guessing that he was amused and maybe even titillated by some of what I was writing. In our workshop, however, on a spring afternoon in 1968, he read aloud and praised the last story I wrote for him. He liked the female character, and he especially appreciated the dialogue. "Rosie Baby" turned out to be my first published short story—it appeared in the Fall 1969 issue of *The Georgia Review*. Even there, I wrote a very gross scene in which the narrator of the story, an American soldier, breaks a Vietnamese child's leg.

I've come to think of him as Peter rather than Mr. Taylor. Probably it's because I'm older now than he was then—it's as if I've aged into peer status with him. At any rate, in my mind now, he's my older-brother fiction-writer; whereas if I'm remembering our time together at U.Va. in 1967 and '68, he's the wise teacher, and I'm the boyish student. It's also the case that, over the years, I've learned more about who he was then. Though it was my privilege to study with one of the American masters of the short story, I didn't have a clue. When we met, I hadn't heard of him and hadn't read any of his fiction. He just seemed to me an old-fashioned gent who liked to read stories by Chekhov and Katherine Anne Porter aloud in class. After I'd been his student for a while and felt an obligation to try out some of his work, I found it way too dry for my taste. I gave up without even finishing the first story in *Happy Families Are All Alike*. It reddens my face to think of that now— because as I've gained a literary education and developed some taste, I've learned to appreciate the subtle mastery of Peter's fiction.

Peter knew a great deal more about me than I did about him. Not only had he lived through being a young male writer—and maybe he'd even been a little ignorant and arrogant, too—but he'd also spent time in a place called Meadows of Dan, which he understood to be pretty close to my hometown of Ivanhoe, Virginia. I think his family had owned a summer place in Meadows of Dan. So from that experience, Peter was claiming part-time status as a Southwest Virginian, somebody who had an insider's knowledge of the kind of people I came from.

That was always a particular interest of his, where people came from and the kind of people they were. When I heard Mariflo say those words, "I wonder when David's going to get around to writing about the good people...," I suddenly realized that Peter must have been puzzling over that question from the moment he read the first short story I handed him. As time went on, he must have been feeling it in an increasingly pained kind of way, because even in my second book of short stories, *Only the Little Bone*, where I finally got around to writing about my family and townspeople, there was a notable absence of "good people." The squalid parts of my autobiography were what most appealed to me as writing material—e.g., a hired hand who rubs poison ivy into the inside of a boy's mother's bathing suit.

Peter must have been hoping for many years that I'd break through to a level of maturity (or generosity) in my writing. Mariflo—who has in fact written quite charmingly about those good people among whom both of us grew up—must also have been hoping for a similar development on my part. As a matter of fact, I took Peter's words to be a charge from both him and Mariflo to get going on the project. What he said added some additional guilt to my normal load—I've always felt both guilt and pride about the trashier aspects of what I write. It also seemed a worthwhile assignment for me to carry around in my mind—"write about the good people of Southwest Virginia."

Well, you write what you write. Both Peter and Mariflo would understand that. It may happen yet. There's certainly no shortage of good people in my memories of growing up in Ivanhoe, Virginia. In my boyhood, I experienced more than my fair share of kindness and—what should I call it?—maybe *grace*, of a peculiarly Southwest Virginia variety, the kind of thing where an older person recognizes that a boy is behaving like a jackass but puts up with it anyway in the knowledge that boys generally have to behave like jackasses in order to make their way to manhood and so this older person lets the failure go with a kind of high-lonesome smile that informs the boy that he could do better but that he's loved anyway. I know about such goodness, I really do, and I think it should be written about at least as much as poison ivy being rubbed into bathing suits. I'm grateful to both Peter and Mariflo for reminding me of the possibility of writing about good people. But what it all comes down to is that you write what you write, and I'm pretty sure I haven't yet completed the assignment.

"Backstory" is my most recent fictional visit back to autobiography. It's a section of a novel that I've tried to fashion into a short story. Since the main character is female, and nothing in it is anything I actually did, its level of historical truth is somewhere around fifteen or twenty percent. But to me it feels a lot more autobiographical than that because so much of it has to do with a high school student's riding a school bus back and forth between a country hamlet and a small town. About a thousand hours of my adolescence were spent with my butt parked in a school bus seat—and I'm here to tell you that it was positively and negatively character-forming. School bus time is a big chunk of my own "backstory." A question I've addressed with this writing is how does an experience like that affect a person's future if he or she is of an intellectual/artistic inclination? Or how does such an experience "sit with" such a person in adulthood? These are unanswerable questions, which is part of what makes them appealing to a fiction writer, but in my writing, I feel as if I gained some insight. The ambivalence that my protagonist feels about her background is something I feel I've clarified—partially and temporarily—for myself in this writing.

So where in this piece of writing are those good Southwestern Virginia people? Well, Peter and Mariflo, they must be sitting quietly and unnamed in other parts of the school bus. Their paragraphs and pages didn't get written. It's not that anybody here is all that "bad." It's just that my writing still doesn't seem to be locating much in the way of goodness, let alone goodness of a regional variety. And I had the charge with me when I wrote "Backstory." I really did think about Peter's words during the weeks that I worked on this piece. What can I say? I did my best and still didn't get it done.

Here's the insight that's come to me in writing *this* piece. The goodness that Peter and Mariflo assigned me to write about may find its personification in the people of Southwest Virginia, but where I have to discover it first is within myself. "Backstory" testifies to an ongoing obsession of mine—betrayal. I write about it (which is to say that I confess it) again and again. It goes way back. And I have to think that the ultimate aim of such writing/confessing is forgiveness—setting things right. So Peter's message that Mariflo delivered to me really is a bit of well-wishing—a well-disguised prayer. They'd like for me to write my way through this burdensome, squalid obsession. They'd like me to reach my destination—a place where I can forgive myself for whatever crime or crimes I've committed that set me on a lifetime writing journey of confessing one fictional betrayal after another. Words that may at first have seemed a disturbing judgment were actually generous wishes directed to me from the good hearts of my brother and sister story-writing Southwest Virginians.

Backstory

BY HERSELF, IN HER OFFICE with the door shut, Professor Nelson finds that she thinks about her childhood. It happens often enough that she's become aware of it. And it's involuntary. With the door open, she can be up in the Art Department all day long, meeting with students and colleagues, preparing for classes, even just sitting at her desk and thinking about a piece of sculpture she wants to write about, and her past will not intrude. The instant she shuts the door to get a little privacy, it's like she stepped into a time capsule and got herself transported back to the exact place she'd never choose to visit.

Suzanne grew up in the far-back boondocks—nine miles west of the Blue Ridge Parkway, unmarked on all but the most detailed maps—Stevens Creek, Virginia, an unincorporated pocket of houses with a store in the middle and a filling station on the highway at each end. By the people of its neighboring communities, it was regarded as a hostile place. The people who lived there didn't deny it. During most of Suzanne's childhood, Stevens Creek had two or three times as many of its young men serving time in the penitentiary as it had students attending college.

Unfriendliness seemed to be in Stevens Creek's air or water, but Suzanne was never that way. Quiet as she was, she nevertheless always wanted to be close to somebody. Her inclination was to be companionable. Her two older sisters, Bonnie and Gail, started being unfriendly to her when they were all three little. Even nowadays, Suzanne sends them birthday cards, and they don't send her one; at Christmas Suzanne buys gifts for them and their kids, and they send neither gifts nor thank-you notes.

Her parents are friendly toward her, but in a superficial way. They're guarded in their dealings with her—they call only to inform her of a death or serious illness in the family. When Suzanne calls them to chat, she senses how they maneuver to end the conversation.

These estrangements hurt Suzanne's feelings. She's done nothing to cause her sisters' unfriendliness to her, nor has she ever given her parents cause to be wary of her. How could she help being the freak of the family? She didn't even realize she was smarter—a lot smarter—than her sisters and her parents until she was in eighth grade. That's when she had to start riding the school bus thirty-five miles a day to and from the consolidated high school. The teachers there who'd taught Bonnie and Gail were so stunned by Suzanne's ability that they told her: Compared to her sisters, she was a genius. Compared to most of the children who rode the bus in from Stevens Creek to Galax, Suzanne was a female Einstein.

She doesn't have a mountain accent—her intuitive intelligence obliterated it, starting with her first day of eighth grade. People in Galax had a more sophisticated version of Appalachian English than people in Stevens Creek. The way the town kids mocked the country kids was so ruthless that most of Suzanne's Stevens Creek school bus acquaintances became predictably hostile and all the more determined to hold onto their mother tongue. Suzanne was the only one she knew who began adapting.

It was a talent she had—listening, analyzing, imitating. By her sophomore year, the only ones mocking her way of speaking were a few of the more surly Stevens Creek kids who took her Galaxized speech as a sign of betrayal. Mostly, though, the Stevens Creek kids thought of her as the one of them who could compete in that school, the one who had a chance of beating the Galax snobs at their own game.

Nowadays Suzanne is pretty certain that the main reason she changed her speech was so that she could make friends among the smart kids. It didn't work. She was popular—again and again she found herself in groups of Galax girls; she was invited to spend the night at this girl's house and that one's. She made an effort to cultivate the intimacy of several girls she admired, but real friendship never happened. She came to see how jokes and manners and the slangy small talk of the day were actually ways of pushing people away. Stevens Creek boys didn't ask her out because she was too smart; Galax boys didn't ask her out because she lived eighteen miles away. Her remembrance of that time in her life is like a nightmare with her frantically running toward some familiar boy or girl who smiled and beckoned but who seemed to be sucked backward through space, so that no matter how exhaustingly she ran, she could never close the distance.

There was, however, The Mute. The Limeberrys, his family, had lived on the outskirts of Stevens Creek, for as long as anybody could remember. But The Mute had a foreign look to him, dark skin, converging eyebrows, a beaklike nose, eyes whose whites caught your attention. The Mute looked Middle Eastern. He could speak, but there was a nasal harshness to his voice—it sounded like his words were squeezing through some weird little tube up behind his nose. From his first day of first grade, he'd been brutally teased. By fourth grade, he'd shut up. He shook his head when his teachers called on him. He'd do that, shake his head yes or no, if you politely asked him a yes-or-no question. He did his homework, all of it printed in a neat hand. When he absolutely had to communicate with a teacher, he printed a quick note and carried it to the teacher's desk. The Mute also learned to fight well enough—that is, he could exact enough pain—to convince the school bullies to lay off him. Thus he became a completely isolated boy. In his classes and on the playground, in the cafeteria and the hallways, he moved among the children, but no one spoke with him. No one, as his teachers and the school administrators put it, *interacted* with him. He wasn't even antisocial, as far as anyone knew; he just didn't carry out spoken intercourse with anyone. The Mute made himself almost invisible.

David Huddle »»»»«««« 59

What transpired between Suzanne and The Mute, at the time, seemed to her just something that happened. In retrospect she thinks it was maybe the most significant single moment of the five years she attended Blue Ridge High School. That first August morning of eighth grade, when she got on the school bus behind Bonnie and Gail—of course they'd pushed ahead of her—there was no place to sit. She couldn't know it then, but for a Stevens Creek kid, the most ferocious politics of high school life had to do with where you sat on the school bus. So there she was, standing at the front, one step past the driver, looking down the aisle all the way to the back, and there was no place for her. There were places, but they were window seats being saved by the kid sitting on the aisle. She was going to have to ask somebody to scoot over and give up a saved seat. Among all the faces staring at her, there wasn't a friendly one. Bonnie and Gail had each had a pal who'd saved a seat; now they sat staring at her, too, with that gleeful look Suzanne recognized as pure sibling vengefulness. She felt her face reddening. She was twelve years old and maybe the youngest kid on the whole bus, she had on her new first-day-of-school dress, she didn't think there was anything wrong with how she looked, but there was no way she could make somebody give her a seat if they didn't want to. She glanced back over her shoulder. The bus driver was waiting for her, watching in his mirror to be sure she sat down before he started the bus moving. Twenty-some pairs of eyes blazed at her. She was about to open her mouth to let out what she knew would be a yelp, a wail, a shriek, a moan. That was when The Mute scooted over and gave her a place.

When she had settled into the seat he had given her, she murmured, "Thank you, Elijah." She didn't say what any other kid would have, "Thanks, Mute." She was taking a chance to speak his whole name instead of the nickname "Lige," that she somehow knew he wanted to be called. From far back in school, when he was still willing to speak, she must have remembered his telling someone that was his name. Since first grade, they'd been in the same classroom. She remembered a whole catalogue of humiliations he had suffered from their schoolmates over the years. She'd never spoken cruelly to him or done him any harm, but she'd also never tried to help or defend him. She was his witness. That was what she meant to convey by calling him by his full and proper first name—that and her extreme gratitude, which "Lige" would not have signaled. "Lige" was merely "Thanks," whereas "Elijah" was "Oh my dear schoolmate, I can never adequately thank you for the noble gesture you just made in that most painful moment of my twelve years of life." And her gratitude was only slightly diminished by her suspicion that he had taken the seat-saving aisle-position to avoid the shame of having every bus rider turn down the open seat beside him.

She thought about Elijah while she sat beside him for the long ride toward Blue Ridge High School. The consolidated school held more people in its interior than lived in the entire hamlet of Stevens Creek and its surrounding sub-hamlets of Rakestown and Slabtown. And the prospect of what would happen in that huge brick building was worth considering, but it was mostly Elijah she thought about. What kind of parents name their child "Elijah"? Well, she knew what kind. Religious. And she thought about Elijah's last name—Limeberry. She couldn't imagine how people ever got to be named Limeberry, and in her concentration on such matters as his family and his name and the history of suffering that had produced his silence, Suzanne received—as if it were a divine revelation—a blast of empathy: She could feel exactly what it was—even down to the thuds of his heartbeat, his breathing, his body odor, his flat butt on the vinyl seat, and his dozens of thought-out but unspoken remarks—to be Elijah Limeberry. The transmission of that boy's life into her life lasted no more than about fifteen seconds, but it gave Suzanne a brief spasm of shivers.

So for the five years until they graduated they rode the school bus together each morning. They didn't ride together on the way home in the afternoon—and they both understood why that was the case. Suzanne got out of sixth period with enough time to make it onto the bus and claim her own seat. If she'd chosen to sit with Elijah or if he'd chosen to sit with her for that second time in a single day, they'd have been accused of being *"in love."* She understood the absurdity—and maybe even the kindness of it: The bus kids allowed them the morning ride together because it was necessary—it was what they had to do to survive, and every kid riding with them understood that. But they wouldn't tolerate Suzanne and Elijah openly choosing each other's companionship.

So now, when she got on the bus, Elijah automatically scooted over to the window seat to make room. He got into a way of sitting over there, curled away from her and everyone else, that gave him a pocket of privacy. He did something with his notebook over there. Suzanne didn't make much of that—most kids did their homework on the bus. For a lot of them it was the only time they ever did homework. Suzanne herself always read on the bus, though it was usually a book that didn't have anything to do with her classes. She read, and he did whatever he did over there. That was how it was— because within a few weeks after that first morning, they had settled into an unsentimental acknowledgment of their arrangement. She even found herself occasionally slipping back into thinking of him not as "Lige" or "Elijah," but as he was called by everyone else on that bus—The Mute. And Elijah had gone back to meeting her eyes only for the small moment each morning when she got on the bus, and he scooted over. There were no further exchanges.

Later on, Suzanne would wonder if Elijah hadn't done something to catch her attention. That morning on the bus—for whatever reason—she had happened to glance over that way. At the time it seemed a coincidence: She didn't mean to look at his notebook, and he didn't mean to reveal it. What he'd drawn astonished her: A boy struggled with a monster before a crowd of faces. In her momentary view of the picture, Suzanne saw that the struggling boy was Elijah and that hers was a face at the front of the crowd. In the picture he'd even drawn her fingers touching her mouth to suggest concern and horror. The other faces were fixed in demonic grins. The monster, however, was the dominant image, many-eyed and many-handed, a dark gluey mass of slime that evidently could wrap itself around the boy, could take hold of his arms, legs, neck, and torso, could envelope him in utter shadow. Quite clearly in their struggle, the monster would prevail. And the boy's—Elijah's—face held an expression of noble determination. One fist was poised for a blow toward a set of the monster's eyes. The other hand pushed away a grasping set of dark fingers. But anyone could see that the fight wasn't going to last more than an instant or two longer. Elijah was about to be consumed by the slimy darkness.

Because she couldn't take her eyes away, Elijah caught her staring at the picture. Their eyes met and held for an uncomfortable few moments—as if he'd caught her secretly trying to hurt him, but of course she hadn't been doing that at all. And what transpired between them in the look? Even now, Suzanne can't think of a name for it, but it was something like a contract: He agreed to let her know that picture drawing was what he did, and she agreed not to talk about it with anyone. Well, of course there were no words to the understanding, but that had to be it because she never told anyone, and Elijah did allow her, from time to time, to see the pictures he drew. What she really wanted was to see him drawing, but he never did that in front of her. If she were looking, he would only make a minor addition or shading. When he was concentrating, he turned away from her and curled himself over the notebook—as if he accomplished the drawing within some secret cavity of his body. He worked with a blue pen and a black pen, and sometimes when his shoulders made a certain movement, Suzanne was pretty certain he was switching from one pen to the other.

As Suzanne recalls it now, she realizes that there was a complicity between them that she didn't even think about at the time. She had to help Elijah keep his secret. So if he revealed a drawing to her, he had to do so in a way that wouldn't allow any other kid to see it. And she had to be unobtrusive in her looking. Actually, in the hundreds of mornings they rode the bus together, he probably showed her only a dozen pictures. But when he did, the two of them had to shield that picture from being seen by kids on the bus around them. What amazes her now is that even as intricate as the whole arrangement was, she seldom thought of it after she stepped off the school bus. Perhaps in the mornings, as she stood by the roadside waiting for the bus to pick them up, she wondered what bizarre vision Elijah might have to show her today. But during her school day and while she was at home, there was no place in her thoughts for Elijah "Lige" Limeberry, a.k.a., The Mute. It was as if she stashed him away in some compartment of her mind.

That remembrance disturbs her now because it wasn't all that simple. What was it about those long ago days that nags at her? At first she can't grasp it, but as she pushes her memory of Elijah, she begins to take hold of it. She didn't think about Elijah because it made her uncomfortable to do so, but she did think about his pictures. Except "think" isn't the right word for it. His pictures lingered in her mind. They were just there—is that right? Well, even now, she holds vivid images that she knows were drawn by Elijah's hand. Except that isn't right either, because several of the black and blue images in her mind in those days—and that she holds in mind nowadays, as well—were not drawn by Elijah. Suzanne herself made them up.

She began to see certain parts of her daily life in terms of Elijah's pictures. Or she remembers pieces of her experience as if Elijah had drawn them.

In particular, one day at lunch, there was a fight between two Galax boys, football players, in which the one ripped the other's shirt down the front, and the other stood screaming foul names and brandishing a cafeteria chair. It was T. W. Ballard and Jason Sunenblick. Suzanne saw them fight, and she knows Elijah didn't see it—because unless the weather was freezing cold, he always took his brown bag outdoors to eat by himself. But she remembers that fight as if Elijah had drawn it, the fighters looming huge and furious, Jason's veins popping in his neck as he stood cursing. T. W. Elijah would have shown the faces in the background—maybe one of them hers—and he would have shown the vice-principal pushing his way through the crowd to stop the fight and take the boys to the office, even though that didn't literally happen.

The actual pictures Elijah showed Suzanne were always related to school. He drew one that she sees so clearly in her memory that it's as if it were a painting she had studied and written an article about—it was of Mrs. Childress, the librarian, standing at her desk and checking out a book for a huge boy behind whom there was a line of equally huge boys and girls waiting to bring books up to the librarian's desk for her to check them out. There were other high school student giants sitting at tables in the background, some of their faces recognizable to Suzanne. In this picture, Mrs. Childress, drawn mostly in blue, was a miniature human being in comparison with the great oafs, drawn in heavy black lines, who surrounded her in the library. Elijah perfectly captured the woman's precarious authority over them all. He'd invested her with blue beneath black lines so that the blueness was like an energy held within her. It was as if even in her smallness, the librarian was the finished human being, whereas the students were the gawky, blank-faced, doofus creatures who didn't know what to do with themselves and who depended on petite Mrs. Childress to bring momentary focus to their lives. The one at the front of the line wore the face of Lee Shinault, a boy famous for his unruly behavior in school, a boy who defied teachers and administrators but who was known to revere Mrs. Childress. Suzanne is sure that only she and Elijah ever really noted the unacknowledged stature of that woman in the school and that she—Suzanne—wouldn't have known how to describe it. But once Elijah had set it into a picture and allowed her to see it, she could grasp what she already knew.

There was a stretch of time in her senior year, however, when Elijah showed her no pictures and when he seemed to stop noticing her altogether. The place beside him was available each morning—he no longer sat on the aisle side, pretending to save it, because by that time, it had long been established that the place was hers. Also, he'd stopped catching her eye then or at any other time during the bus ride or the school day. In the general chaos of her life in those days, however, the change in Elijah's behavior was barely noticeable. Occasionally Suzanne wondered if she'd done something to anger him or hurt his feelings, but she couldn't think of anything. She couldn't even be certain that there was any change in him. Other matters were demanding most of her attention. She'd gotten caught up in applying to colleges and discussing scholarships with her guidance counselors and teachers. Blue Ridge High School had taken on the mission of helping Suzanne Yarborough go on to higher things than were available to her in Stevens Creek or Galax.

One cold January day when she got on the school bus, she found the seat empty, Elijah not there. Everyone on the bus seemed to be staring at her in a moody silence. Elijah never missed school. Something made Suzanne glance back at the bus driver. His eyes were on her, too—in the mirror that let him monitor what went on behind him. "His mother died," the driver said very quietly. "She'd been sick a long time." Suzanne nodded but said nothing. She merely took her seat. And the bus driver said no more. He let the clutch out and started the bus moving as he always did. She didn't dare scoot over to the window—even with him not there, it would have been wrong to take Elijah's place.

She sat with her book bag in her lap, the same as she did every morning with him sitting beside her.

The more she thought about him, the more her face burned with shame. That his mother had died seemed to her horrible, though as she tried out the idea, she didn't mind imagining her own mother's death. But if she'd been a friend to Elijah as he'd been to her that first morning, she'd have found out why he'd been holding himself away from her all that time. Or she'd have just known—she who had once actually felt exactly what it was like to be Elijah! Everybody else on the bus—though they said nothing—seemed to have known. All that time he'd been sitting beside Suzanne, he'd needed her to know his mother was ill, but she'd been thinking of herself and her future and the days of magical freedom that lay ahead of her at college. When she noticed how quiet the kids around her were, she also noticed that tears were falling down her cheeks and splashing onto her book bag. That embarrassed her so that she turned toward the window and curled around herself the way Elijah did when he was working in his notebook. As she sat like that, it happened to her again, that sharp blast of empathy, which was like a magic trick in which she lived in Elijah's body and mind for about twenty seconds. It made her face burn all the more.

All that day in school and on the bus home and in her dealings with her parents and her sisters—all of them leaving her completely alone now that they knew she was making her escape to college within the year—she was preoccupied with what she should do. Before her mother called her down for dinner, she even sat in her room trying to draw a picture that would show her embracing Elijah to comfort him in his grief. But she had no talent for drawing, and even if she could have drawn it, the picture would have been all wrong. She had no desire to embrace him—she just wanted to let him know she felt his sorrow, or that she was somehow with him in his sorrow, or that she wanted to be with him. The more she sat staring at her feeble attempts at making a picture, the more confused she became about exactly what she wanted to convey to Elijah. By dinnertime, however, as she ate with her family—who mostly talked among themselves as if she weren't there with them—she reconciled herself to writing him a note. There wasn't anything else she could do. She couldn't draw, she certainly couldn't give him a hug, and she knew it would put him in an impossible position if she spoke to him. So when she finished washing the dishes—which was the chore that when she was around eleven had fallen to her by mutual agreement among the other members of her family—she went upstairs to compose her note to him. She paced her room, she did some of her homework, she read in the library book Mrs. Childress had recommended to her, and she composed draft after draft of her note of condolence. No matter what she wrote, she hated the words, and so she finally settled on writing the thing she hated the least, which, as it turned out, was the most impersonal version of what she felt she had to say.

> Dear Elijah,
>
> I am so sorry about your mother. Please forgive me for not having spoken to you about her before this. I know this must be a terrible time for you, and I hope you will let me know if there is anything I can do to help make things easier for you.
>
> Your school bus friend,
Suzanne

She had the note ready to give him the next day, but once more he wasn't in his seat on the bus. That was a Friday, and the funeral—she had learned from the biweekly county newspaper, *The Mountain Sentinel*—would be held on Saturday. She even considered attending it—she could walk to the church—but she decided it would be a mistake to make a statement like that to her family and to the townspeople. For both her and Elijah, it would be a source of humiliation for months to come. She was pretty certain he would be on the bus on Monday morning; that would be when she could discreetly pass the note to him. All through the weekend, she agonized, but she always came up with the same answer: She couldn't act like she didn't know what had happened, she couldn't draw a picture for him, and she couldn't speak to him; therefore, she had to give him the words she had written.

Monday morning Elijah was back in their seat, on the window side with his face turned toward the glass. When Suzanne sat down, he didn't turn toward her or make any sign. The note was folded in its envelope and tucked into an outside compartment of her book bag. She'd planned out exactly how to pass it to him. Through the next two stops she waited until Leonard Branscomb was stepping up into the bus; Leonard was a tall red-faced farm boy who always had funny things to say to his pals in the back of the bus. Suzanne waited until he was passing directly beside her, carrying on as usual and distracting everyone on his way to the back. That was when she turned toward him and said quietly but definitely, "Elijah," within a few inches of his ear. She witnessed the jolt of startlement she caused him. When he cast his eyes back at her, she pushed the envelope against his hand, positioned so that he could see that she had written his name on it. He took it and met her eyes once more in a look that struck Suzanne as fearful. *Why should he be afraid of me?* was the thought that lingered in her mind as he turned back toward the window, curling around himself in that way that he always did.

The relief she felt at having delivered the note into his hand was such that she excused herself from worrying any further about him or what he would make of what she had written. She opened her library book, and with her eyes directed toward the page, her mind began savoring a vision of herself walking across a campus in springtime—

Radford College or maybe V.P.I. She would be wearing new clothes, she would be in the company of a boy or a friend, she would have the admiration of her professors—

That was when she heard her name in a belch of sound, as if it had been croaked by a whale or a porpoise trained to use human speech. Turning, she found herself staring straight into Elijah's tear-streaked face. He grasped her hand that was nearest him, tugging it and holding onto it long enough that Suzanne thought she was going to have to pull it back away from him to get free. He uttered two more syllables—"Thank you"—as if he were talking through his nose but loud enough that the kids sitting near them would have had to hear him. He was staring at her with those weird whites of his eyes gleaming in his head. Then he must have sensed how repulsed she was by his behavior, because he suddenly released her hand and jerked himself back around toward the window, raising the same hand that had grasped hers to swipe at his wet cheeks and eyes.

What she had to do was—she knew this as clearly as if it had been written before her eyes in letters of fire—TOUCH HIM. But what she wanted to do more than anything was move away, get some distance between his flesh and hers. Of course there wasn't another seat she could have taken, and she probably wouldn't have moved even if a place had been open. But she also couldn't will herself to put a hand on his arm or shoulder or knee, couldn't force even a whispered *I'm sorry*. All she could do was sit where she was, locked into her sitting-on-the-bus-with-her-bookbag-on-her-lap posture. The moment passed when he would have allowed her to touch him; she began to sense that if she even brushed him with her fingers, he'd strike at her in anger. Her face blazed with shame.

That was when she heard the noise from the seat from behind them and across the aisle—stifled laughter. She guessed that the ones sitting there—Becky Stoots and Mildred Coleman—were talking about what they'd just seen happening between her and Elijah. She could turn back toward them and give them a look, but that would make it worse. If you made a spectacle on that bus, as she and Elijah had done, you had to expect ridicule. So she sat where she was, hoping he would understand she meant to endure the humiliation with him. But she knew he wouldn't see it that way. He'd see it correctly: She'd betrayed him. She'd written and delivered that note to him to make herself feel better. And when he'd responded openly, she'd pulled away from him. So if it was possible to make Elijah Limeberry's life worse—the life of a friendless boy who'd been harshly mocked from his very first day of school and whose mother had just died—that was what she'd done. That was how she'd repaid his kindness of rescuing her on her first day of riding the bus.

Suzanne knows this episode is at the core of what she protects from her acquaintances who want to know where she came from and what it was like to grow up in Appalachia. But this is not all there is to it. There are probably forty or fifty old betrayals and humiliations from those days that radiate around that one moment on the bus with The Mute. Suzanne can bring back an amalgamation of smells that come from that bus, from the Colemans and Stootses and Yearouts and Blairs and Branscombs and Mabes and Davises and Groscloses who got on at such and such a stop. Some of those children were clean, but most seldom bathed and their clothes were rarely washed. One or two sat among them with the fragrance of fried side meat still clinging to them. The Porter children came straight onto the bus from milking cows and slopping hogs. She can probably even bring back the exact fragrance of Mildred Coleman's hair spray after she'd gotten caught in the rain—the memory of that scent oddly thrills Suzanne when it comes back to her. From her hundreds of mornings and afternoons on that school bus, she can bring back snapped bra straps and cruelly flipped ears and ripped shirts and thrown condoms and tampons and curses and names called and blows struck and even the time Leonard Branscomb spat in the face of Buntsy Russell and dared him to do anything about it. And there was Botch Arnold pulling a sharpened beer can opener from his sock and threatening Trenton Mabe with it—that memory is such a squalid little treasure that Suzanne knows she will never let go of it. Though she has devoted the major energy of her life to putting them behind her—to denying them—these people nevertheless remain an essential part of who she is.

But it isn't so much the squalor or ignorance or ugliness of that former life that Suzanne wants to conceal. It's certainly true that she looks back on all those people now as she looked into the tearful face of The Mute—with involuntary revulsion and contempt. That's what she should be ashamed of, but that isn't quite all of it. It's that she knows she's locked in this—how to name it?—*posture* of halfhearted empathy. All she had to do was despise Elijah Limeberry like everyone else; he'd have understood that, and she'd have caused him no pain. All she has to do to separate herself from her past is—cleanly and completely—to despise it. She can't do it. However much she yearns to, she won't ever be able to do it.

He paid her back. When she thinks of it now, Suzanne grimaces. Whether or not payback was all he intended, she'll never know. It was on one of her last days of school, when she was still giddy from the offer of a full scholarship from Hollins College. She'd applied to Hollins only to appease the English teacher who was the most passionate among the group of school people pushing her to get a college education. And it was the full scholarship offer that turned her parents away from resisting her going to college. When they found out she could go for free—and could even work at the library for spending money—they had to stop saying that they weren't about to pay good money for her to go off to some fancy college just to come back home and turn up her nose at them. That spring of her senior year in high school, it was as if she'd turned a corner in her life, and now she was strolling down some grand boulevard of possibility and opportunity. The episode of her treachery to Elijah was fading from memory, and she had only a few more days of riding the school bus before she'd be finished with it forever. She and Elijah had continued sharing a seat, but they both understood that it was for the sake of deflecting interest away from them. If she'd sat elsewhere, their bus comrades would have teased them without mercy. So when she took her seat in those last mornings, Suzanne endured the discomfort she felt emanating from Elijah, and she supposes he must have endured whatever feelings were emanating from her—though it troubles her to name what her feelings were. She tells herself, *Sorrow—I felt sorry for what had happened between us*—but the truth of it is that she *loathed* him. Now that she had betrayed Eliajah as she had, what she had to endure sitting beside him was loathing of such an intensity that she must have reeked of it, like the smell of cow manure that came onto the bus with the Porter kids.

The grimace that comes to Suzanne's face now—twenty-two years after the fact—is located almost entirely in her discomfort with that feeling. Not that she thinks loathing is an unacceptable feeling, but that she felt it for a boy in whose body and mind she actually lived for a total of about thirty-five seconds. And for a boy whose kindness saved her in a desperate moment.

What The Mute actually did was to leave an envelope with her name on it stuck in her locker door on the last day of school. He must have been paying close attention to her and planning carefully because it was the last time she'd ever open that locker. And she wasn't going to ride the bus home that afternoon because she'd been invited to spend the night with Robyn Hanks, who was also going to attend Hollins that fall and who said she wanted to get to know Suzanne a little better. When Suzanne saw the envelope, she knew immediately

David Huddle ⟫⟫⟫⟪⟪⟪ 73

who'd put it there—it was exactly like the envelope she'd passed to him that morning on the bus, except that this one had SUZANNE printed on it in black ink. She dreaded reading the note so much that she carried it into the girl's bathroom, and though there wasn't a soul in there at the end of the school day, she even took it into a stall before she opened the envelope.

It was a folded card of good stationery—the same as she'd used to write her note to him—and when she unfolded it, the inside was entirely inked over. But that wasn't entirely it either. While Suzanne stood in the shadowy little box with the toilet—and the smell of girl's bathroom getting to her now and causing her to feel slightly nauseated—she realized that there was blue ink beneath the nearly solid blackness. The black pen strokes left just enough space between them for a vague blue shape to be discernible. She had to leave the stall and carry the notecard to the window to study it in bright light. And still she couldn't make it out. There was something back there, and she thought it was probably a face, but she couldn't be sure about that. The no-image image nagged her to study it even more carefully— she thought about looking at it at home with a magnifying glass. But as she stood there by the window holding that card, something about the thing began to anger her. Something sparked in her. She ripped it! Then she ripped those two pieces into four. Those two rippings happened in an instant, before she'd even thought about it, and she stood holding the quartered parts. Finally she took them with the envelope over to the big trash can, where she ripped everything into pieces the size of snowflakes. She let them fall into the can, and she took special care to be certain that the "SUZANNE" from the envelope was so thoroughly shredded that not even a genius of a puzzle worker could have reassembled it into a readable pattern.

That was maybe the first time Suzanne had ever deliberately destroyed anything. Leaving the rest room and walking out of the school building toward the parking lot to meet Robyn Hanks, she was shocked at how exhilarated she felt. Her hands still tingled with the ripping. *That was good,* she thought, as the school door clanged shut behind her. *That was just fine,* Suzanne thought as she hurried toward the girl who wanted to get to know her better.

Reginald Shepherd

REGINALD SHEPHERD's first book, *Some Are Drowning*, was published by the University of Pittsburgh Press in 1994 as winner of the 1993 Associated Writing Programs' Award in Poetry. Pittsburgh published his second book, *Angel, Interrupted*, in 1996. His third collection, *Wrong*, was published by Pittsburgh in 1999. Shepherd is the recipient of a 1993 "Discovery"/*The Nation* Award, a 1995 NEA creative writing fellowship, a 1998 Illinois Arts Council poetry fellowship, and a 2000 Saltonstall Foundation poetry grant, among other awards and honors. He lives in Ithaca, New York, and is an assistant professor of English at Cornell University.

Thirteen Ways of Looking at Alvin Feinman

>>>>>>>>>>>>>>>>>>>>>><<<<<<<<<<<<<<<<

I.

I've never been much mentored in my life. Like the people living without a presiding deity in Stevens' "Sunday Morning," I've inhabited an island solitude, unsponsored, free of all artistic patronage. It's not that I wouldn't have welcomed such: like some academic flying Dutchman, for years I sailed from school to school, program to program, in search of a true mentor. (And of course, to avoid having to get another job doing data entry.) I have had professors from whom I've learned, who have taught me valuable things about my work (sometimes intentionally, sometimes inadvertently or even against their will); but few who were truly formative, and fewer still who were consistent in their attention. And I confess that I've never been much of a protégé, even in potential; I have opinions and convictions, or at least obstinacy and willfulness. In my experience, those in a position to be mentors want to break you and remake you, if not in their own image then in their image of who or what you should be. Most have seemed more interested in the breaking than in the remaking, like children losing interest in a new toy they've smashed. Perhaps because I lived for seven years with a vicious stepfather who was determined to break me (he broke my mother: she died), I've never had much taste for being broken, and I've put too much effort into making myself to hand the job over to someone else. There's no guarantee, after all, that the new version will be an improvement, and much evidence to suggest that it will be distinctly worse. At the least it won't be mine, and I've always been perhaps too proprietary about my *self*: it has, usually, been all I had.

II.

I have, however, had one person in my life who could truly be called a mentor. Alvin Feinman was my thesis tutor at Bennington College, a tiny arts-oriented college in a tiny very non-arts-oriented town in Vermont. He never "did anything" for me but help me write better poems; he never did anything to me but force me to see that however pleased I was with something I'd just written, it could always be better, had to be better if I were to call myself a poet. For Alvin, to be a poet was always an aspiration, not something one could claim to *be*. I think if I'd have asked him he would have said, "I would *like* to be a poet."

III.

Several years before we worked together on my thesis, I passed Alvin (Bennington's was a very small campus; one was always passing someone) and he asked what I was reading. At the time I was immersed in minor, late modernist writers, like Léonie Adams, Sidney Keyes, Genevieve Taggard, and Marya Zaturenska. They were very "poetic" writers, and that appealed to me at a period when I liked my poems to come festooned with giant neon letters that spelled out "I AM A POEM" in alternating primary colors. Alvin dismissed them with a wave of an almost certainly cigarette-bedecked hand (Alvin always had a cigarette in his hand, and the yellowed fingertips to go along with it). He asked me why I wasted my time on trivia: "I don't read much poetry, but everything I read is great." Milton, Blake, Wordsworth, Shelley, Keats, Stevens, and Hart Crane: only the immortals were worth one's time. Alvin didn't read widely: he read *deeply*. He could spend an hour on a short lyric of Blake's and make you see it as if no one had ever read it before. I, who compulsively "keep up" with what's being published now, who don't go back nearly as often as I should to the writers who first inspired me to write (Yeats, Eliot, Stevens, Crane, Auden), often hear his voice in my head and feel chastened. For Alvin, there was no point in reading a poem unless it was great and no point in writing a poem unless it (not you: it) at least aspired to greatness.

IV.

By the time, several years later, that Alvin became my senior thesis tutor, I had developed an unhealthy desire to write about my life, or rather, since I had no life to speak or write of, about my feelings and the fantasized life (tragic but beautiful) I could have been leading if I weren't leading my own lame excuse for one, and I wanted to write about that imagined life of mine in fairly demotic language, though a highly festooned and over-dressed demotic. (I've never lost my taste for flash and neon, scarlet and miniver.) I was rebelling against poetry, doubtless as a result of having read too much Léonie Adams. (Luckily I'd also read Louise Bogan, so I still remembered there was an alternative within "poetry.") I was perhaps also rebelling against my own rebellion against the still-reigning aesthetic of transparency. Sometimes even the most stubborn intransigent wants to relax and write, "I look out / the window / and I am / important." For Alvin, you were always the least important thing in your poem (a lesson most contemporary poets have never learned), and a story was only as good as the metaphors it could give rise to, could become. Anything can tell a story; only a poem can raise story into metaphor. "Too unmetaphorizable" was one of the most damning phrases in Alvin's vocabulary; "This achieves true metaphor" was one of his greatest praises.

V.

Since I've begun teaching I've noticed that one is expected always to praise, to be "supportive," rather like a bra or a jock strap. One of my current students told me I should always give out equal amounts of praise and criticism, which meant that I should always lie at least a little. There may be good in every person (or maybe not), but there is definitely not good in every poem. This student also told me always to accept students' work on its own terms. (This was a young man full of foolish advice, and fuller still of himself.) Alvin felt it his duty to tell me not only whether I was doing something well, but whether it should be done at all. He warned against the dangers of "fluency über alles," as he called it, of doing something simply because you can or simply because you want to. (What you want has no place in poetry, he believed; it's what the poem wants.) He once said of a poem I showed him that he saw little in it but my desire to write a poem, and he saw accurately.

VI.

Alvin told me he was more unsparing with me than with his other students because he respected my work; it was worth the effort to take my poems seriously. While I have as much of an appetite for praise as anyone (probably more), I welcomed Alvin's criticisms because he understood my poems and what they were trying to do. Sometimes he understood them better than I did. My work had been praised, admired, appreciated, but before Alvin it had never been understood. His criticisms sometimes stung, but I recall the anecdote Ezra Pound tells of showing his *Canzoni* to Ford Maddox Ford, who rolled on the floor in laughter. "That roll saved me years of bad writing." Unfortunately I still had some years of inadequate writing ahead of me, but I can't blame that on Alvin—he did his best with the material at hand. In any case, he would never have condescended to anything as undignified as rolling on the floor.

VII.

One of my projects as a high school and a college poet was to recuperate and regenerate the language and *topoi* of chivalric love for love between men. (I had projects when I was younger and more ignorant. Now I don't know what I have.) Alvin once told me he had found many of my poems baffling and opaque until he changed the pronouns; then he saw my attempt to recoup a particular vocabulary and syntax of love. He explained to me what I was trying to do. (The various projects of my youth were often somewhat inchoate.)

VIII.

Alvin was especially alert to the occasions when a poem failed to live up to its own possibilities, when it fell away from the finer revelations it proposed into the quotidian. Usually the poem failed by settling for the merely personal, revealing the writer rather than the word. For

Alvin, one's interest in oneself had no place in poetry, and in his poems one will find not face but mask. But it's a mask far more alive than the greatest mass of mere faces.

IX.

Just as the blackbird moving in and out of Stevens' poem, its motion defining the field of vision, makes sight possible, so Alvin made me see poetry as if for the first time. John Hollander wrote over thirty years ago that "Feinman's poems are perhaps the most difficult of [his generation]. Their difficulty is not that of allusion, nor of ellipsis, nor of problematical form, however, but the phenomenological difficulty of confronting the boundary of the visual and the truly visionary."

X.

Alvin and I agreed that the great failure of contemporary poetry was its abandonment of the modernist project, a failure that began with the turn of the post–World War II poets (Lowell, Bishop, Jarrell, etc.) to the merely personal and local, a willful turn toward the *minor*, as if the larger questions of word and world with which the modernists struggled were both impossible to face and somehow gauche to bring up in polite company. I saw it as my duty to continue the lapsed project of modernism, as Alvin did in his own poetry. It's no accident that the one person I can call a mentor is also one of my favorite poets, and the true inheritor of Hart Crane, though the high standards he set for himself may well have come to make poetry impossible for him. As he recently told me, "Poetry is always close kin to the impossible, isn't it?"

XI.

Harold Bloom on Alvin's first and, for all intents and purposes, only book, *Preambles and Other Poems:* Feinman seeks to become Necessity, "to write the last possible poem, a work that takes the post-Romantic consciousness so far as to make any further advances in self-consciousness intolerable" (*The Ringers in the Tower*). I once asked Ben Belitt, another marvelous and underrated poet, and another Bennington teacher of mine (it was he who told me how important it was to let oneself lie in poems: 'truth' and 'honesty,' while they might make the writer feel good about himself, were beside the point in a poem), why he thought Alvin had never written another book. "Well, I think he just wrote himself into a black hole. There was nowhere else to go." That black hole (whole?) is, I think, Mallarmé's Nothing of the white page, Yeats's fascination of what's difficult become the impossibility of poetry. Like Mallarmé, Alvin was one for whom the desire for perfection brings its own defeat, and like Mallarmé, Alvin had no terror of the void. His laconic defeat is worth a thousand garrulous victories over the silence from which words come and to which they return. As Bloom writes of Alvin's poems, "their difficulty is their necessity."

XII.

Alvin was completely indifferent to, even disdainful of, the world of publishing, of self-promotion and publicity. While he was my thesis tutor Alvin received a letter from John Hollander, editor of the Contemporary Poetry Series at Princeton University Press, expressing great admiration for his work and soliciting him for a new manuscript. Alvin asked me what I thought he should do about this request. To me the answer was obvious, but to him it really didn't matter. (I think he found something slightly vulgar about seeking publication and recognition. He'd had a certain amount of acclaim early in his career and apparently had found it wanting in substance.) In the end Alvin agreed to reprint *Preambles* with a handful of more recent poems, which is what Princeton did in 1990, in a volume entitled simply *Poems*. I admire Alvin's indifference to the blandishments and proffered rewards of the world, but would never choose to emulate it. That is probably a weakness of mine, though it is, fortunately or not, a useful weakness.

XIII.

I graduated from Bennington College in 1988 (four years after I should have: another long sad story). My thesis was a collection of poems that very eventually and rather drastically mutated into *Some Are Drowning*, my first book. In June of 1994 President Elizabeth Coleman and the college's board of trustees initiated what has come to be called the Great Bennington Faculty Massacre, also known by the more gullible or the more cynical as a bold educational experiment. A third of the faculty were terminated, with no opportunities for early retirement, and tenure was abolished. Alvin was among those summarily fired, ostensibly because he was no longer an active "practitioner," in fact because he was a leader in resistance to Coleman's determination to run the college without faculty input. Her goals were to destroy faculty governance at the college and to eliminate anyone who had ever challenged her. Bennington's spin doctors managed to present this violation of academic freedom and due process as a new vision of higher education, and indeed it is, one in which faculty, no matter how long and loyal their service (no one taught at Bennington for the pay!), no matter the brilliance of their accomplishments, are simply contract workers, utterly expendable and to be disposed of at the administration's will.

Alvin Feinman was certainly not expendable to my experience of Bennington College, but the college I attended no longer exists. Luckily for me and for the world of poetry, Alvin most emphatically still does.

Interglacial

White of extinct god's etch and simmer
spills from salt heaven, pluvial
law of breakage suffering
away from himself, throat kissed
shale black. (Shall I compare thee,
incommensurate, and greet you as
a god, good substitute? Lie
still and let me listen to your skin.)
Hieratic wrack having attained
the age of representation, refutation:
see him so water, so clearly dissolved.

He wonders if he might be the visible,
spontaneous prosody of gesture,
recurrent, irretrievable, and only in part
a god, part of a god: belief fragment
worn smooth by glaciers in retreat,
abraded by the Pleistocene to glimmer,
shine, scuttle and glyph luster. Odor
of artifice, odor of lies
down in the teeming interior seas,
salt flats of Lake Bonneville
where water was slept away.

Erin McGraw

ERIN MCGRAW was a Stegner Fellow in Fiction at Stanford University from 1988 to 1990. She is the author of two collections of short stories, *Bodies at Sea* (University of Illinois Press, 1989) and *Lies of the Saints* (Chronicle Books, 1996). Her stories have appeared in *The Atlantic Monthly, The Georgia Review, Story, The Southern Review*, and other magazines. She teaches at the University of Cincinnati.

Complicate. Simplify.

The best writing teacher I've ever had was also the best-dressed teacher I've ever had. The point is not trivial. John L'Heureux believes in the importance of the workshop, the dignity of the students' and teacher's shared endeavor, and he dresses to demonstrate his respect. Heavy, lustrous shirts, buttery ties, jackets that cup his shoulders like soft hands. In wardrobe as in literature, John appreciates good tailoring and fine material.

He was my teacher in the late 1980s, at Stanford University. Word was already out among writing students that a class with John was like nothing else. He bore down on stories, I heard. He half-memorized them. He brought the full weight of his classical education to his students' small attempts. Those students too readily pleased with their own words writhed their way through workshops that examined the ways the writer had overestimated the success of a paragraph, a scene, a story. John wasn't an insulting teacher or an aggressive one, but he expected students to work with all their strength, and he had more strength than most of us.

"What is this scene doing?" he might ask pleasantly in the book-lined, dusty room where the class met.

"I think it's obvious. The scene illustrates the character's loneliness."

"Yes, but what is it doing? At the beginning of the scene he hasn't made up his mind. At the end of the scene he still hasn't made up his mind. What structural purpose does it serve?"

After class students who felt ill-used gathered at the campus bar. Craft, craft, craft, they complained. Structure, structure, structure. As if that's all that fiction is. I listened, but kept my mouth shut. Even when I felt stung and under-appreciated—pretty much every week— I had a dim sense that John was driving me toward a specific goal, and his goal was bigger and better than any I had constructed for myself.

Besides, the gripers were wrong. John did not demand well-structured stories for the sake of structure alone. According to his conception, every scene—every sentence—needed to advance not just plot, but also characterization, moral complexity, tone. By writing in this way, choosing every word to advance several effects, we would be forced to test our ideas and refine our vision. Craft was a means to an end, and the end was to write fiction wiser and more profound than any of us could be in our daily lives.

I was abashed by such an ideal, which seemed so steely in comparison to the wooly way I'd been working: by hunch, by guess, by the clear blue sky. John forced me to examine my hunches, a process that was exhausting for him and embarrassing for me. Confronting one of my particularly messy stories, he made an outline, blocking out each scene (thirteen of them in sixteen pages) and showing where it went. Mostly, nowhere.

"Every scene needs to build, to move the action forward," he said, and then added advice he often gave in class: "Complicate the motive. Simplify the action."

Most writers, and certainly most readers, will appreciate the acuity of this advice. In life we don't take action, particularly interesting, unwise action, for a single reason. We don't rob the cash register only out of greed, but also out of self-pity, fear of our own cowardice, and the image of our mother, bedridden and apt to die if she doesn't get her expensive medication soon, even if we spend the money on a trip to Aspen. Motives rarely come neatly or single file.

What readers might not understand so quickly is the difficulty of trying to adhere to this dictum. It is hard enough to create believable characters, interesting setting, well-tuned prose, and all the rest of it. But to squeeze a character until all of his several desires and impulses lead him to a single inevitable and yet surprising action calls on a writer's whole intelligence and insight and steel-clad imagination. It's not surprising that many writers, daunted by the high stakes, fold.

I do so myself, at least twice a week. But now that John's stamp is on me, work that settles for simple motive and complex action looks fussy and thin, timid at the core. A character does or doesn't answer her phone. She does or doesn't take a walk. She has many sensitive thoughts. She does or doesn't make dinner, go to a bar, go home with an old chum. In the end, she wakes up and thinks that life is strange and unknowable. Please.

I don't see any reason to bother writing if we aren't trying to make stories that engage fundamental issues. That statement, of course, indicates a belief that fundamental issues exist—about the nature of human will, for instance, or the endurance of evil. John believes in such issues, and so do I. And so when I'm at my best I gather up my efforts and courage and try again to complicate the motive, simplify the action.

In "Ax of the Apostles," I think I come close. The story is dear to me in part because I can see John's imprint on it so clearly. Proud, irritable Father Murray is set in opposition to his heedless student, Adreson, a runner. At first Father Murray's bullying intellect seems more than a match for Adreson's mere vigor. But by the end of the second scene Father Murray's shameful weak spot—a raging sweet tooth, unappeasable physical appetite—is exposed, and from that point each scene intensifies both Father Murray's vulnerability and his bitterness. He and Adreson become locked in a kind of prize fight (the metaphor is John's), both of these men of God intent on eradicating his enemy. By the final two scenes, Father Murray crashes to an unwelcome new level of self-awareness, and in a mixture of compassion and rage—*complicate the motive*—sets out in a single gesture—*simplify the action*—to give Adreson the same gift.

Some writers will find such a schematic breakdown distasteful, arguing that it reduces the story to mere system. Myself, I don't see anything wrong with systems. Humans have circulatory, endocrine, and skeletal systems, and they don't stop us from having love affairs, defrauding employers, giving all our possessions to the poor. Our systems permit us to do these interesting things, and systems in fiction perform the same function. Once the fuzzy, half-thought-through actions (I'm thinking of my own worst impulses here) are either taken out or sharpened, once the hard questions about motivation are engaged, once every scene is made to advance the characters' situation both emotionally and practically, then a story is finally unencumbered enough to reveal essential realities with both force and nuance.

Or so it seems to me. The classical structure John taught puts the needs of the story above the needs, desires or ego of the writer, and so it is a goal that is just as hard for me to attain with the fiftieth attempt as it was with the first. But working in this fashion I come to prize the effort itself, the weirdly voluptuous joy of pursuing the almost unattainable, jumping to grasp what is barely within my reach. Sometimes I get up from my desk with muscles trembling. If I'm feeling grand, I think of Jacob wrestling with the angel at Peniel, an encounter from which Jacob emerged limping, blessed with soul-expanding knowledge of no practical value. John would, I hope, laugh at that, an exact metaphor for art, a story both complex and simple.

Ax of the Apostles

AFTER FOUR HOURS SPENT locked in his office, gorging on cookies and grading sophomore philosophy papers, Father Thomas Murray seethed. His students, future priests who would lead the church into the next century, were morons.

"Kant's idea of the Universal Law might have made sense back in his time, but today we live in a complex, multicultural world where one man's universal law is another man's poison, if you know what I mean." So there are no absolutes? Father Murray wrote in the margin, pressing so hard the letters were carved into the paper. Peculiar notion, for a man who wants to be a priest.

They didn't know how to think. Presented with the inexhaustibly rich world, all its glory, pity and terror, they managed to perceive only the most insipid pieties. If he asked them to discuss the meaning of the crucifixion, they would come back with Suffering is a mystery, and murder is bad. Father Murray looked at the paper before him and with difficulty kept from picking up his pen and adding, *Idiot*.

He had planned on spending no more than two hours grading; he would do well to go over to the track and put in a couple of overdue miles. But flat-footed student prose and inept, flabby, half-baked student logic had worked him into a silent fury, and the fury itself became a kind of joy, each bad paper stoking higher the flames of his outrage. He reached compulsively for the next paper in the stack, and then the next, his left hand snagging another of the cookies he'd taken last night from the kitchen. Not good—lackluster oatmeal, made with shortening instead of butter—but enough to keep him going. What makes you think, he wrote, that Kant's age was any less complex than yours?

Still reading, he stretched his back against the hard office chair, which shrieked every time he moved, and started to count off the traits lacked by the current generation of seminarians: Historical understanding. Study skills. Vocabulary. Spelling. From down the hall he heard a crash and then yelps of laughter. "Oh, Alice!" someone cried. Father Murray closed his eyes.

A month ago one of the students had sneaked into the seminary a mannequin with eyelashes like fork tines and a brown wig that clung to its head like a bathing cap. Since then, the mannequin had been popping up every day, in the showers, the library, at meals. Students mounted it on a ladder so that its bland face, a cigarette taped to its mouth, could peer in classroom windows; twice in one week Father Murray had had to look around to see why his students were giggling. Now a campaign to turn the mannequin into the seminary's mascot was afoot. Savagely, Father Murray bit into another bad cookie, then stood, inhaled, and left his office.

At the bend in the hallway, where faculty offices gave way to dormitory rooms, five students clustered beside an open door. The mannequin, dressed in towels, half-reclined in the doorway to Quinn's room. Blond, morose Quinn, a better student than most, tugged the towel higher up the mannequin's bosom. The customary cigarette had fallen from the doll's pink plastic mouth and now dangled by a long piece of tape. "You should have seen your face," Adreson was saying to Quinn. Father Murray knew and loathed the sort of priest Adreson would become: loved by the old ladies, peppy, and brain dead. "I thought you were going to faint. I thought we were going to lose you."

"Jumped a foot," added Michaels. "At least a foot."

"Went up like a firecracker," Father Murray suggested, and the seminarians turned, apparently delighted he had joined them.

"A Roman candle," Adreson said.

"Like a shooting star," Father Murray said. "Like a rocket. Like the *Challenger*. Boom."

The laughter slammed to a halt; Adreson stepped back, and Father Murray said, "You men sound, in case you're interested, like a fraternity out here. I would not like to be the one explaining to the bishop what tomorrow's priests are doing with a big plastic doll. Although I could always tell him that you were letting off some steam after your titanic academic struggles. Then the bishop and I could laugh."

"She fell right onto Brian," Adreson murmured. "Into his arms. It was funny."

Father Murray remembered a paper Adreson had written for him the year before in which Adreson had called Aquinas "The Stephen Hawking of the 1300s," not even getting the century right. In that same paper Adreson had made grave reference to "The Ax of the Apostles." From any of the other men Father Murray would have allowed the possibility that the citation was a joke. Now he looked at his student, twenty years old and still trying to subdue a saddle of pimples across his cheeks. "You have developed a genius for triviality."

"Sorry, Father."

"I'm giving you a piece of information. Think about it."

"Thank you, Father."

"Don't bother thanking me until you mean it."

"Oh, I mean it, Father." Adreson pursed his mouth—an odd, old-maidish expression. "Sorry we disturbed you. Guess we're too full of beans tonight. Hey—you want to go over to the track?"

Father Murray felt a plateful of oatmeal cookies churn in his stomach. "Another time. I've still got work to do."

"*Corpore sano*, Father."

Father Murray snorted and turned back toward his office. He cherished a measure of low satisfaction that the one Latin phrase Adreson seemed to know came from the YMCA slogan.

HE SHOULD, OF COURSE, have taken up Adreson's offer. By ten o'clock his stomach was violent with oatmeal cookies; his error had been in eating even one. As soon as he'd tasted that first sweet bite, it was Katy bar the door. Tomorrow he would have to be especially strict with himself.

Strictness, as everyone at St. Boniface knew, was Father Murray's particular stock-in-trade. Fourteen months before, his doctor had called him in to discuss blood sugar and glucose intolerance. "You have a family history, is that right?"

Father Murray nodded. His mother—bloated, froglike, blind. Groping with her spongy hand to touch his face. He had held still, even when she pressed her thumb against his eye, and hadn't said a word. "Doesn't everybody have a family history?" he said.

"This is no joke. You are at risk," the doctor said. "You could start needing insulin injections. Your legs could be amputated. You could die. Do you understand that?"

Father Murray considered reminding the doctor that a priest's job entailed daily and exquisite awareness of his mortality. Nevertheless, he took the doctor's point: Father Murray's forty-five-inch waist, the chin that underlaid his chin, his fingers too pudgy for the ring his father had left him. If he let the disease take hold he would deteriorate in humiliating degrees, relying on others to walk for him when his feet failed, to read to him when the retinopathy set in. A life based wholly on charity—not just the charity of God, which Father Murray could stomach, but the charity of the men around him. The next day he began to walk, and a month later, to run.

For a solid year he held himself to 1,100 exacting calories a day, eating two bananas for breakfast and a salad with vinegar for lunch. His weight plummeted; his profile shrank from Friar Tuck to Duns Scotus, and the waist of his trousers bunched like a paper bag. The night Father Murray hit one-fifty, ten pounds below his target weight, Father Radziewicz told him, "You're a walking wonder." They were standing, plates in hand, in line for iced tea. Father Radziewicz's eye rested on Father Murray's piece of pork loin, slightly smaller than the recommended three ounces, stranded on the white plate. "How much have you lost now?"

"One hundred twenty-four pounds."

"Enough to make a whole other priest. Think of it."

"I'm condensed," Father Murray said. "Same great product; half the packaging."

"Think of it," Father Radziewicz said. His plate held three pieces of pork, plus gravy, potatoes, two rolls. "I couldn't do it," he added.

"It's just a matter of willpower," Father Murray said. "To the greater glory of God."

"Still, isn't it time to stop? At least slow down. Maybe you've glorified God enough."

"I've never felt better in my life."

The statement was largely true. He had never in his life been quite so satisfied with himself, although his knees sometimes hurt so much after a twelve-mile run that he could hardly walk. He bought Ibuprofen in 500-count bottles and at night, in bed, rested his hand on the bones of his hips, the corded muscles in his thighs. Out of pure discipline he had created a whole new body, and he rejoiced in his creation.

So he was unprepared for the muscular cravings that beset him shortly after his conversation with Father Radziewicz. They came without warning, raging through the airy space below his ribcage. The glasses of water, the repetitions of the daily office, all the tricks Father Murray had taught himself now served only to delay the hunger—five minutes, fifteen, never enough.

One night he awoke from a dream of boats and anchors to find himself pushing both fists against his twisting stomach. Brilliantly awake, heart hammering, he padded around the seminary, glancing into the chapel, the storage room that held raincoats and wheelchairs for needy visitors, the pathetically under-used weight room. Finally, giving in, he let his hunger propel him to the kitchen, just so that he'd be able to get back to sleep. Holding open the refrigerator door, he gazed at cheesecake left over from dinner. He was ten pounds under-weight. He had left himself a margin; probably he was getting these cravings because he actually needed some trace of fat and sugar in his system. And the next day he could go to the track early and run off whatever he took in tonight. He ate two and a half pieces of cheese-cake, went back to bed and slept as if poleaxed.

Since then Father Murray had hardly gone a night without stealing downstairs for some snack-cookies, cake, whatever the seminarians and other priests, those wolves, had left. He stored his cache in a plastic bag and kept the bag in his desk drawer, allowing himself to nibble between classes, in the long afternoon lull before dinner, whenever the hunger roared up in him. Twice he broke the hour-long fast required before taking Communion; each time he sat, stony faced, in his pew, while the other priests filed forward to take the Host.

At meals he continued to take skimpy portions of lean foods; sometimes he was so stuffed with cookies even the plate of bitter salad seemed too much to get through. Father Bip, a Vietnamese priest he had often run with, told him that he was eating like a medieval monk. Father Murray slapped himself hard on the rump. "Brother Ass," he said. That rump was noticeably fleshier than it had been two months before, and he vowed again that he would recommence his diet the next day. That night, anticipating the stark hunger, he quietly walked the half-mile to a drug store and bought a bag of peanut butter cups, several of which he ate on the walk back home.

As he lay in bed, his teeth gummy with chocolate and peanut butter paste, his days of crystalline discipline seemed very close. The choice was simple, and simply made; he remembered the pleasure of a body lean as a knife, a life praiseworthy and coherent. Yet the next night found him creeping back to the kitchen, plastic bag in hand, not exactly hungry anymore but still craving. Already his new black pants nipped him at the waist.

AFTER HIS ONE O'CLOCK Old Testament class the next afternoon, Father Murray returned to his office to find Adreson waiting for him. The young man, who had been absently fingering a flaming blemish beside his nose, held out his hand toward Father Murray, who shook it gingerly and ushered Adreson into his office.

"How was your class, Father?"

"We entertained the usual riotous dispute over Jerome's interpretation of 2 Kings." Then, looking at Adreson, he added, "It was fine."

"Your O.T. class has a real reputation. Men come out of there knowing their stuff."

"That's the basic idea."

"Sorry. I'm nervous, I guess. I want to apologize for making all that racket in the hallway last night."

"Thank you."

"I knew we were being—"

"—childish," Father Murray offered.

"—immature. I just thought you should know that there was a reason. Brian's mother has multiple sclerosis. He just found out last week. She's at home by herself with four kids, and she keeps falling down. I know it's killing Brian, but he won't talk about it. He just keeps going to class and services. It isn't healthy. That's why we put Alice in his room."

"He may find it comforting to keep up his usual schedule. This may be his way of coping," Father Murray said, autopilot words. Genuine shock kept him from asking Adreson how a towel-wrapped mannequin was supposed to help Quinn manage his sorrow.

"He needs to talk, Father. If he talks to people, we can help him."

"You have a lot of faith in yourself."

"We're here to help each other." His hand fluttered up toward his face, then dropped again. "If it were me, I'd want to know I could count on the guys around me. I'd want to know I wasn't alone."

"He prays, doesn't he? He may be getting all the support he needs. Not everything has to be talked out."

"We're not hermits, Father."

"That is abundantly true."

A burst of anger flashed across Adreson's face, and Father Murray leaned forward in the chair, which let out a squeal; he was more than ready to take the boy on. But after a complicated moment Adreson's mouth and eyes relaxed. "Of course you're right. I thought I should apologize for disturbing you." He straightened, clearly relieved to have put the moment behind him. "I'm going for a run this afternoon. Want to join me?"

"You're doing a lot of running lately. I'd suggest you take a few laps around the library."

"You're great, Father. You don't ever miss a lick." He pulled up another grin from his ready-made, toothy stockpile. "Track meet's coming up. I'm running the relay and the 440. 440's your event, isn't it?"

"Distance," Father Murray said.

"I'm a little obsessed about that 440. Sometimes in practice I can get close to the conference record, so now it's my goal: I want to break the record, put St. Boniface in the books."

"Generations of the faithful will thank you."

"I'll have plenty of time to be pastoral later. Right now, running's the best talent I've got." He winked. "I know what you're going to say: Not a very priestly talent, is it?"

"I wasn't going to say anything like that. You are the model of today's seminarian."

Father Murray waited for Adreson to leave the office before he swiveled to gaze at the maple outside his window. Hundreds of tender spring leaves unfurled like moist hands, a wealth of pointless beauty. Where, he wondered, was Quinn's father? Had he run off after the fifth child, or had he died, snatched away in midbreath or left to dwindle before the eyes of his many children? Cancer, heart attack, mugging. So many paths to tragedy. Now Quinn's mother, trapped inside a body that buckled and stumbled. Before long she would rely on others to cook for her, drive for her, hold a glass of water at her mouth.

"Too much," he muttered, his jaw so tight it trembled. He didn't blame Quinn for not wanting to talk to Adreson, who knew nothing about pain, which he believed could be eased by conversation. He didn't have a clue of sorrow's true nature or purpose: to grind people down to faceless surfaces, unencrusted with desire or intent. Only upon a smooth surface could the hand of God write. Every priest used to know that. Father Murray knew it. Quinn, bitterly, was learning it.

Father Murray hit his leg with his fist. Turning to the desk, he began to reach for the stale cookies in his drawer, then pushed back his chair. If an overdue visit to the track hurt, so much the better. He couldn't take on any of Quinn's suffering, but at least he could join him in it.

WEEKS HAD PASSED since Father Murray had last gone for a run; his legs were wooden stumps, his breath a string of gasps; he flailed as if for a life preserver when he rounded the track the fourth time. Adreson, out practicing his 440, yelled, "Come on—pick 'em up, pick 'em up!" and Father Murray disinterestedly felt his dislike for the boy swell. After six laps he stopped and bent over. Adreson sailed around twice more. Father Murray waited for his lungs to stop feeling as if they were turning themselves inside out, then straightened and began again.

At dinner he stood in line for a slice of pineapple cake. "Oho," said Father Bip. "You are coming down to earth to join us?"

"I should be earthbound after this, all right."

"Should you be eating cake?" Father Radziewicz asked. "Wouldn't a piece of fruit be better?"

"Of course it would be better, Patrick," Father Murray snapped. "Look, one piece of cake isn't going to make my feet fall off."

Father Radziewicz shrugged, and Father Murray stomped across the dining room to a table where Father Tinsdell, a sharp young number imported this year from Milwaukee to teach canon law, was holding forth. "You're all thinking too small. We can sell this as an apparition. Trot Alice out after Mass and get the weeping women claiming that their migraines have gone away and their rosaries have turned to gold. We'll have the true believers streaming in. Pass the collection basket twice a day; next thing you know, we're all driving new cars. We'll buy one for the bishop, too."

Father Antonin leaned toward Father Murray. "He found the mannequin in his office. Hasn't shut up since."

"The women are always grousing about how there isn't enough of a feminine presence in the church," Father Tinsdell said. "Well, here they go. Five feet, six inches of miracle-working doll. We can put her in the fountain outside. Stack some rocks around her feet: Voila! Lourdes West. Bring us your lame, your halt. If enough people come, somebody's bound to get cured. That should keep us rolling for the next century."

"You know," Father Murray said, setting his fork beside his cleaned plate, "Rome does recognize the existence of miracles."

"Somebody always stiffens up when you start talking marketing." The man's face was a series of points: the point of his needly nose, the point of his chin, the point of his frown set neatly above the point of his cool smile, directed at Father Murray. "Don't get in a twist. I'm up to date on church doctrine."

"People have been cured at Lourdes."

"I know it." Father Tinsdell leaned forward. "Have you ever seen a miracle?"

"Nope," said Father Murray.

"There are all kinds of miracles," Father Antonin broke in. Without even glancing at the man, Father Murray knew what was coming: the miracle of birth, the miracle of sunrise, those reliable dodges. He looked at Father Tinsdell. Father Point.

"Never. Not once. You?"

"Yup. Saw a fifteen-year-old girl pull out of renal failure. She was gone, kidneys totally shot. Her eyeballs were yellow. Even dialysis couldn't do much. For days her grandmother was in the hospital room saying rosaries till her fingers bled. She got the whole family in on it. And then the girl turned around. Her eyes cleared. Her kidneys started to work again."

Father Murray stared at the other man. "That can't happen."

"I know. But I was there. I saw it."

Father Murray pondered Tinsdell's mocking gaze. How could a man see a miracle, a girl pulled from the lip of the grave, and still remain such a horse's ass? "I envy you," Father Murray said.

"Keep your eyes open. No telling what you might see." Father Tinsdell stood. He was thin as a ruler. "I'm getting some more coffee. Do you want more cake?"

"Yes," said Father Murray, though he did not, and would ignore the piece when it appeared.

SEVERAL TIMES IN THE NEXT WEEK Father Murray paused outside of Quinn's door, his mouth already filled with words of compassion. But Quinn's door remained closed, separate from the easy coming and going between the other men's rooms. Father Murray respected a desire for solitude, the need for some kind of barrier from the relentless high jinks of all the Adresons. He pressed his hand against the door frame, made ardent prayers for Quinn's mother, and left without knocking.

He should, he knew, have saved at least one of those heartfelt prayers for himself. His hunger was becoming a kind of insanity. Food never left his mind; when he taught he fingered the soft chocolates in his pocket, and at meals he planned his next meal. Nightly he ate directly from the refrigerator, shoveling fingerfuls of leftover casserole into his mouth, wolfing slice after slice of white bread. He dunked cold potatoes through the gravy's mantle of congealed fat, scooped up leathery cheese sauce. He ate as if he meant to disgust himself, but disgust eluded him. Instead, he awakened deep in the night, his stomach blazing with indigestion, and padded back to the kitchen for more food.

In the dining room he carried on the pretense of lettuce and lean meat; his plate held mingy portions of baked fish and chopped spinach unlightened by even a sliver of butter. He ate as if the act were a grim penance. For a week now he hadn't been able to button the waist of his trousers.

One night after dry chicken and half of a dry potato he made his ritual pause outside of Quinn's door, then continued down the hall to his own room. Fourteen papers on the autonomy of will were waiting, and promised to provide ugly entertainment. But when he opened his door he jumped back: Propped against the frame stood the mannequin, wearing his running shoes, his singlet and jacket, and his shorts, stuffed with towels to hold them up. From down the hall came a spurt of nervous laughter, like a cough.

Father Murray waited for the laughter to die down, which didn't take long. Adreson and three other men edged out of the room where they'd positioned themselves; they looked as if they expected to be thrashed.

"My turn, I see," Father Murray said.

"We didn't want you to feel left out," said Adreson.

"Well, heavens to Betsy. Thank you."

"We thought you'd like the athletic motif. It was a natural."

"An inspiration, you might say."

"I was the one who thought of having Alice running," Adreson said. "Some of the other men suggested your clothes. Hope you don't mind." He leaned against the wall, hands plunged into the pockets of his jeans. The others, relaxed now, ringed loosely around him.

"Did Quinn have suggestions for this installation?" Father Murray looked at the mannequin's narrow plastic heels rising from his dirty running shoes, the wig caught back in his dark blue sweatband, the face, of course, unperturbed.

"Didn't you know? He's gone home to help out." His voice shifted, taking on a confiding, talk-show-host smoothness. "I don't think it was a good idea. His mom may be getting around now, but over the long run, he needs to make arrangements. Immersing himself in the situation will give him the sense that he's doing something, but he isn't addressing the real problems."

"Maybe he wants to be there."

"Not exactly a healthy desire, Father. Multiple sclerosis, for Pete's sake. I don't want to be brutal, but she isn't going to get better."

"No," Father Murray said.

"But you know Brian. He said he had to go where he's needed. I told him that he has to weigh needs. He needs to ask, 'Where can I do the most good.' He can't fix everything in the world."

"You weren't listening to him. Every need is a need," Father Murray said, chipping each word free from his mouth. "If you're hungry and you remember that children in Colombia are starving, do you feel any less hungry?"

"Sure. When I'm on vacation I always skip lunch and put that money in the box. And you know, I never feel hungry. Never."

"One of these days," Father Murray began, then paused. His voice trembled, surprising him; he felt quite calm. Filled with distilled, purified hatred for the boy, but calm. "One of these days you'll find that your path isn't clear. Choices won't be obvious. Sacrifices won't be ranked. Needs will be like beads on a necklace, each one the same size and weight. It won't matter what you do in the world—there will still be more undone."

"My dark night of the soul." Adreson nodded.

"Your first experience of holiness," Father Murray corrected him. Adreson flattened his lips, and his friends looked at their shoes. "Zing," Adreson said.

"Pay attention. I'm trying to get you to see. If you could take on Quinn's mother's disease tomorrow, if you could take it for her, would you do that?"

"We each have our own role to play, Father. That's not mine."

"I know that. Would you reach for this other role?"

Angry, mute, Adreson stared at the carpet. Father Murray understood that the young man was exercising a good deal of willpower to keep from asking, Would you? Would you? and he meant to ensure that Adreson remained silent. If the young man asked, Father Murray would be forced to confess Yes. Yes, I would, his desire caustic and bottomless.

"I'll go ahead and get Alice out of your room, Father," Adreson was saying.

"Leave it for now."

"I'm sorry. It was just supposed to be a joke."

"I know that. I'm not trying to punish you." Father Murray watched the ring of young men shrink away from him. "It's something new in my life. I'll bring it down to your room tomorrow. Besides, I need to get my clothes back."

The men retreated toward the student lounge, where they would drink Cokes and discuss Father Murray's bitterness, such a sad thing to see in a priest. None of them, Adreson least of all, would imagine himself capable of becoming like Father Murray, and in fact, none of them would become like Father Murray. Only Quinn, and he was gone.

Father Murray turned and studied the mannequin, which looked awkward, its angles all wrong. When he adjusted one of the arms, the mannequin started to tip; its center of balance was specific and meant for high-heeled shoes. Quickly he tried to straighten it, but it inclined to the right. In the end, the best he could do was prop the plastic doll against the bureau and berate his painfully literal imagination, which had flown to Quinn. He wondered how often the young man had already steadied his mother on her way to the bathroom or the kitchen. Father Murray's singlet had slipped over the mannequin's shoulder; he pulled it up again.

Adreson and the others must have gotten a passkey and skipped dinner so they could sneak in and rifle his bureau drawers. Father Murray didn't mind—he kept no secret magazines that could be discovered, no letters or photographs. Then he remembered the nest of candy wrappers, the thick dust of cake crumbs. And he himself, talking to Adreson about hunger.

"Mother of God." He paced the room in three familiar steps, turned, paced back. The mannequin's head was tilted so that the face gazed up, toward the flat ceiling light, its expressionlessness not unlike serenity. A bit of paper lingered where a cigarette was usually taped, and Father Murray leaned forward to scrape it off. But the paper didn't come from a cigarette. Carefully folded and tucked above the mannequin's mouth, as precise as a beauty mark, was placed a streamer from a chocolate kiss; when Father Murray touched it, the paper unfurled and dangled over the corner of the mannequin's mouth like a strand of drool, and the doll pitched forward into his arms.

He thrust her back, resisting the impulse to curse. Her balance, he finally saw, was thrown off by extra weight in the pockets of her clothes. The pockets were distended—how had he not noticed this?—stuffed. Father Murray stabilized the mannequin with one hand and rifled the pockets with the other, his heart thundering.

He knew upon the first touch. Handfuls of dainty chocolate kisses, fresh-smelling, the silver wrappers still crisp. His vision stinging, he dropped them on the bureau and let them shower, glittering, around his feet. The air in the room thickened with chocolate; he imagined it sealing his lungs. A full minute might have passed before he fished out the last piece and sank to the floor beside the pool of candy.

Adreson: grinning, amiable, dumb. Seminary record-holder in the 440, possessor of a young, strong body. He didn't look capable of malice. He didn't look capable of spelling it. But above Adreson's constant, supplicating smile sat tiny eyes that never showed pleasure. They were busy eyes, the eyes of a bully or a thug. Eyes like Adreson's missed nothing, and Father Murray had been a fool to think otherwise. He had attributed the nervous gaze to self-consciousness, even to a boyish desire to make good, a miscalculation that might have been Christlike if it weren't so idiotic. Like mistaking acid for milk, a snake for a puppy.

Pressing his fist against his forehead, he saw himself illuminated in the silent midnight kitchen, the overhead light blazing as he shoveled food into his mouth: a fat man making believe he had dignity, and the community of men around him charitably indulging his fantasy. Only Adreson withheld charity.

He fingered the candies on the floor. Unwrapping one, he placed it on his tongue, the taste waxy. He unwrapped a second and held it in his hand until it softened.

THE NEXT DAY, SEATED IN HIS OFFICE at the far end of the hall, Father Murray wasn't able to see Adreson's face when he entered his room. But he knew what Adreson was confronting. The mannequin, clean now of Father Murray's clothes, sat in a wheelchair under the ceiling light. Father Murray had had to break the legs with a hammer to get them to bend; plastic shards jutted like shivs. The head was twisted to the right, a painful angle that made the unengaged expression look like a mask over hidden suffering.

"Vicious. Really vicious. The action of a sick man." Adreson seemed to know Father Murray was listening; perhaps he hoped that others were, too. His voice was loud enough to carry to the end of the corridor. Father Murray clasped his hands and leaned forward, intent on hearing every word his student had to say. "A man like this has no place in a seminary. The bishop won't think so, if he hears. He won't want us to be taught viciousness."

Father Murray shook his head. Once again Adreson was getting his lesson wrong, missing the point. On Father Murray's desk shone a pile of foil. His pockets, his hands, were empty.

Maura Stanton

MAURA STANTON received her BA from the University of Minnesota and her MFA from the University of Iowa. Her first book of poetry, *Snow on Snow*, won the Yale Series of Younger Poets Award in 1975. Her second collection, *Cries of Swimmers*, was published by the University of Utah Press in 1984. Each of these titles has been reprinted in the Carnegie Mellon Classic Contemporary Series. *Tales of the Supernatural* was published by David R. Godine in 1988. Carnegie Mellon published *Life among the Trolls* in 1988 and *Glacier Wine* in 2001.

Berryman and Rutsula:
Two Prototypes

>>>>>>>>>>>>>>>>>>>>>>X<<<<<<<<<<<<<<<<<<<<

John Berryman gave a poetry reading at the University of Minnesota one winter when I was an undergraduate. The auditorium was crowded, but I found a seat near the front. I was excited. I knew Berryman was the real thing, a famous writer who happened to live in Minnesota, an important poet like Eliot and Frost. But he seemed to stumble over his own feet as he approached the podium. At first I could hardly hear him as he mumbled and coughed and peered around at the audience, his veined hands shaking as he held up a book. His eyes were red, his lower lip trembled, his voice shook. He read his poems slowly, his voice cracking, falling to a whisper, rising to a shout. His head, with its strange gray beard, bobbed about as if it belonged to someone else.

My heart pounded. Was this what poets were like? Did writing poetry make you crazy? I slunk away.

Later that year, my internship at an English-language newspaper in Mexico City fell through, and my dream of becoming a foreign correspondent vanished. I'd been counting on a summer in another country to change me from a shy introvert into an intrepid girl reporter. Now I knew that I'd be lucky to get a nine-to-five job in a public relations firm.

I felt trapped. I longed to be a writer, a real writer, not a writer of reports or news releases, but I did not know how to go about it. Every month I bought a copy of *The Writer*, and read articles about how to plot and how to make characters come alive. I'd written half of a suspense novel, but every now and then I'd push my romantic story away in despair, knowing I wanted something more out of writing than escape or money. I'd grab a piece of the yellow paper we used in journalism classes and write a poem about my feelings, a poem full of abstractions and symbols. Then I'd retype the poem on greasy erasable bond, and, following the directions in *The Writer*, I'd send it off to *Mademoiselle* or *The New Yorker*. By the time the blank rejection arrived, I'd be back at work on the novel.

In the spring of 1968 I found out that the English Department had hired a visiting writer for the fall to teach a creative writing course. Excitedly, I signed up.

I was nervous when I walked into the classroom that fall, but Vern Rutsala, a quiet young man with a soft voice who had published his first book of poetry, *The Window*, with Wesleyan, put me at ease. He immediately shifted my attention away from an obsession with the poet's personality to the craft of writing poems.

Vern had assigned Donald Hall's anthology *Contemporary American Poetry*, and when he talked about the poems in class, he did not make them seem mysterious and symbolic. He showed us how the poems worked, how they had dramatic situations, stories to tell, occasions, voices. Two years before I had studied Yeats's "Among School Children" in a literature class. Although I had taken careful notes in the margins as the teacher explained the symbols in the poem, I had no idea what the poem was about. I assumed poems were written in code, or were statements of philosophy. Now, under Vern's subtle guidance, poems began to make sense to me. I read William Stafford's "Traveling Through the Dark" over and over, delighted by the poem's narrative structure, and even though I had meant to write fiction in the class, I started writing poems and turning them into the worksheet for discussion, getting them back each week with Vern's comments in the margin. He'd point out lines he liked, or places where my poem was unclear, so that I could revise it.

Poetry took over my life. Sometimes at night I'd write as many as three poems in one sitting under the tensor lamp, angled to light only my paper and not wake my baby sister, who slept in her crib on the other side of the room.

In January, armed with a new understanding of poetry, I dared to face my bête noire again. I began to audit Berryman's famous Humanities class. I'd sit in the middle of the large classroom, rubbing my hands, still cold and stiff from a long bus ride, as he lectured about the Renaissance. I was both frightened and fascinated by him. He represented centuries of culture and scholarship, a poet-scholar-madman exiled and hounded by the barbarians. When he wasn't the "sixty-year-old smiling public man" from Yeats's poem "Among School Children," he was Crazy Jane made flesh, the terrifying truth-teller, raging and raving.

One day Berryman started to rock the lectern back and forth. He seemed to enjoy the noise and sensation, and kept doing it for five full minutes while we undergraduates sat there with our saucer eyes, enthralled. After the next lecture, gathering all my courage, I approached Berryman and told him I wrote poetry, too. His breath flamed. His hand clawed at my arm. I could see his reddened eyes behind the thick black glasses. Writing poetry was a miserable business, he said. He began to complain bitterly about editors who rejected him. I fled.

It was a relief to sit in Vern's classroom in a circle, talking about line breaks and similes with the other students, some my age, some older. I blossomed as a poet under Vern's mild, gentle praise and unobtrusive suggestions. He was a poet, but he spoke of his wife, Joan, and his children as if he were leading an ordinary life.

All that winter I went back and forth between John Berryman and Vern Rutsala, frightened by one, reassured by the other. In June I was going to graduate, and I'd been interviewed for a job working in the courthouse, an ugly Gothic building that housed the jail as well. I saw myself trapped inside those stone walls for the rest of my life. When I was old I'd start mumbling to strangers on the bus, like the old men reeking of alcohol who climbed aboard in the bad neighborhood, rode a few blocks, and got off again. They looked like Berryman, and perhaps they had poems folded up in the torn pockets of their dirty overcoats with the yellow fleece collars.

One day after class, before I took the bus home, I told Vern how miserable I was, that my life seemed spoiled though I was only twenty-two. I told him that I was on the verge of taking an awful job, but that the only thing that made me happy was writing poetry.

Vern nodded sympathetically. Then he told me the secret. There was a place called the Iowa Writers' Workshop where young people like myself—like himself, for he had an MFA from Iowa—went to study poetry.

Riding the bus home past the ugly courthouse where I was not going to work for the rest of my life, I let myself dream of a small town in Iowa where dozens and dozens of young men and women rented rooms in white frame houses in order to write poems for two years. What happened at the end of two years was a little hazy, but bright like morning fog. I thought about Vern's poem, "The Poet at Twenty-Seven." I wouldn't be as old as that for a long, long time, but when I was, I'd be a poet, too, like Vern, and, God help me, even like Berryman.

Ode to Berryman

"Fame is the spur…"
—Milton

I opened your book today, John Berryman,
And gasped to see you, a "majestic shade,"
Towering over my desk in this cramped room
As if it were your tomb
And you'd returned to make me feel afraid
That I'd forgotten all the poems you made.
When I was twenty-two I watched you loom
Above a hundred students in the lecture hall.

We fidgeted in January gloom
As you balanced there, back against the wall,
Wishing we'd disappear. Who could take notes
About the valiant poets
Of the Renaissance, when ink froze in pens?
Swaddled in coats and hats, our noses red,
We puffed our steamy breath into our scarves,
Half-numb from bus rides, or stalled-out cars.
You stared, I think, in horror,
Exiled, like Ovid, where barbarians roared.

That's when you grasped the heavy podium
And leaned against it with your trembling weight,
Making it rattle. Then nodding your head
Involuntarily like a puppet,
You rattled it some more and started humming,
Involved in your debate
With inner voices that wanted you dead.
We sat there cowering in our bolted chairs,

Afraid of your unmanageable despair.
For five minutes you wobbled before us
And when you stopped there was a gaping hush.
At last you cleared your throat,
And like an ordinary teacher assigned days,
Said who to read, and what to know by rote.

   Because I longed to be a poet, too,
I sidled up to you once after class.
You twitched around so I could smell the booze
Flaming on your breath, removed your glasses,
And scrutinized me while I stammered out:
"I'm reading your poems, Mr. Berryman."
"Good for you, dear. Louise Bogan
Rejected me at *The New Yorker* again.
Do you know why?" I shook my head in doubt
As you pulled out her letter.
"John," you mimicked, "You're not getting better."
You laughed, your forehead clenching up with pain.
"This century sickens me. So am I worse?
Does Vietnam require sublime verse?"

   Two years later at an Iowa party,
You smiled to hear me flatter your ego,
And stroked your veined hand across my knee
In front of your wife, who stared straight ahead
As she perched, shoulders clenched, by the piano,
Her back to the shut keys, her face red.
I knew your value then as a celebrity
Though your strange, anguished lyrics meant little
As I wrote alone in winter, the teakettle
Boiling dry to silence while I thought
Of my own words and images, and wrought

Poems out of nothing. When I heard you'd jumped
Off that bridge into the Mississippi
One cold January, my throat lumped:
I knew the attraction of the frozen waves,
Had felt that stomach-thrilling vertigo
As I brushed against the rail in flying snow
On my way to a detested job that began
At nightfall when the prairie wind saves
And hardens the gray slush.
Then I dismissed you, raving old man
With your theatrical failure and sour lust.
    Today, restless in middle-age,
I paced my empty house, then glimpsed my face
Reflected in a saucepan and felt caged
Inside my wrinkling body's narrow space.
So I was stunned to open this old book
Your *Dream Songs*, and see you yearn and flash
Out of the meter and fast, talky rhyme
Just like some fabulous crook
Imprisoned for life, who wished his pals in crime
Could find the loot he stashed.
    "Action in the midst of thought," you wrote
Picking up two chairs, then tossing them down
Before the undergraduates you hoped
Might somehow preserve your personality
In scribbled diaries
As you played the role of sage or desperate clown.
Our blank looks must have troubled your pose
As you strove for fame even in awkward prose
Written by students with pale memories.
And so I conjure you, John Berryman—

Stand again on that stage
Laboring to vindicate your poems
Through gesture and rage,
And force the world to hear your mortal howl
Though you are far beyond your fading groans
And have become your old friend, Mr. Bones.

Elizabeth Graver

ELIZABETH GRAVER is the author of two novels, *The Honey Thief* and *Unravelling*, and a short story collection, *Have You Seen Me?* Her work has been anthologized in *Best American Short Stories*, *Best American Essays*, and *Prize Stories: The O. Henry Award*. The recipient of grants from the National Endowment for the Arts and the Guggenheim Foundation, she teaches at Boston College and lives in Lincoln, Massachusetts.

A Double Kind of Knowing

>>>>>>>>>>>>>>>>>>>———<<<<<<<<<<<<<<<<<<

When I sit down to start a story—to grab onto whatever slim thread, sidelong image, fragment of speech might take me on a tenuous journey to an unknown place—I try, to the extent that I am able, to banish outside voices from the room. I try, that is, to sweep my mind clean of conscious influence—mentors, critics, reviewers, readers, even friends. I banish much of myself, as well: the meticulous, ordered, analytic, good-girl part of me. I want looseness at this stage, wandering, floppy dream-thoughts, untutored and unkempt. Let a reader into the room and my muscles tense. Ever a good student, I sit up straighter, squint at my computer screen, aim to please. To say that I actually banish all influences would, of course, be a lie; the mere fact that I am writing, say, something called a "short story," something called an "essay," is proof that I carry, even in my most private moments, a dense bundle of influences, too many voices and traditions to track and name. In the early moments of composing a story, though, I resist those influences. Later, in slow stages, I summon them, but carefully—some might even say suspiciously. Part of writing has always included, for me, this delicate dance between shutting out and welcoming in.

Once I have a rough draft, once the world of the story has shown itself to me in a way that feels solid enough for me to grasp, I venture forth. My first readers are almost always people I consider my peers. In college, that meant the group of five people—some students, some older adults—who made up the writers' group I was in. In graduate school, it meant my closest friends in my MFA program. Now that I am in my mid-thirties, it means my friend Lauren Slater, also a writer, and also, as I am, a teacher of writing. Lauren is as tough and insightful a critic as anyone I've ever shared my work with, and she has taught me a great deal. Has she been a mentor, then? I show her my work; she shows me hers. We're the same age. We discuss, in the same breaths as our writing, the messy or mundane details of our daily lives. There is a give-and-take there, a sense of being on equal footing, that makes her less a mentor than a friend, and it is probably for this reason that I go to her first, when the clay is still wet, my own hands uncertain. I could, at the wrong word uttered by a powerful person, abandon the project in a flash.

I am perhaps particularly attune to such issues because my actual teachers, the ones I studied with in school, have been an unusually powerful lot. I am grateful to all of them both for what they taught me and for what they taught me to resist. Their influences come to me in bits of speech, in scrawled writing on the margins of my early stories, in the strength and vividness of their own work. There is Stanley Elkin, cracking jokes and firing off bits of wisdom from his wheelchair, the way he could sum up what was wrong or right with a story in one coiled phrase, the way he could twist a cliché into a new shape and so reinvent the language. "She suffers beyond her means," he said once of one of my characters, a recent college graduate who had her health and a pleasant boyfriend but was tortured by postadolescent angst. "I would never write about someone," Stanley said, "who was not at the end of his rope." While I may define "rope" differently from Stanley, maybe even define "end" differently, he taught me about urgency and pressure in a story, about avoiding easy self-pity, quick sentimentality, pat gestures. In "Surtsey," this may mean that I tried to give Phoebe a wider range of emotions than I might otherwise have done, to make her situation less one-note. I say "may," because the influence is, at this point, nearly subterranean, part of a landscape I can sense but not quite see.

There is Angela Carter, who, like Stanley Elkin, died too early and left a brilliant body of work. She sat in our MFA classroom at Washington University in St. Louis in her red high-top sneakers, white hair wild around her lovely, high-cheekboned, British face. We were workshopping a story I'd written about a lonely, disconnected boy who lusts after his female cousin. A student used the word "incest" to describe the story. "Mightn't we," asked Angela Carter, "call it something nicer, like *transgression*?"—and so pointed out, in the simplest of ways, how the story was about a blurring of boundaries, a pushing of identities, and was asking to be read without the kind of judgment and finality suggested by the word "incest."

There is, too, Annie Dillard, who taught the first writing course I ever enrolled in, when I was a sophomore at Wesleyan University. The summer before I was to study with Annie, I read *Pilgrim at Tinker Creek*, steeping myself in its thick observations and luminous language and stopping (probably too often, for I was young and in need of heroes) to stare at the photograph of Annie on the cover—the halo of blonde hair, the brown clothes, and deeply contemplative, serious gaze. This, I thought, this is who will show me how to be a writer. On the first day of class, Annie marched in, loud and funny, quite pregnant, wearing a bright blue dress and clutching a can of Coke—no delicate nature girl who blended, brown-clad, with the twigs. I remember feeling a twinge of disappointment, a moment of surprise. How was I supposed to reconcile my sense of the voice on the page, the photo on the cover, with this strapping, talky woman pacing the room in front of me?

Though the voice on the page and the person in the room never entirely merged in my mind, I soon saw how Annie's intense powers of observation and love of language were vividly present in the classroom as well. I was only nineteen, but Annie took me (and all her students) utterly seriously as a writer, and so conveyed to me that I should take myself seriously, too, at the same time that I should never lose the sense of play that had brought me to writing in the first place. Sometimes, she could be almost unbearably honest. "This is ruinously sentimental; I couldn't finish it," she wrote on the first piece I handed into her, a poem about an aging dog. On my final group of poems, she wrote, with no apparent irony, "I wonder if I've pushed you enough. You're good enough that you'll always please your teachers, so you have to set your own goals. Which you're doing just fine." "Follow your literary instincts," she went on to advise me, "and don't let Europe distract you permanently. Do go to graduate school so you can prolong entry into the real world—relax after college and keep learning and don't let anyone pressure you to produce *anything*, either money or books, just goof around and keep loving the stuff and don't let them try to make you conform." Wise words, these, warning me of tensions I couldn't, at nineteen, even have begun to articulate myself, though now I know them all too well.

Years later, after the publication of my first novel, *Unravelling*, I was invited back to Wesleyan to give a reading in the Honors College, in the same room where I'd read from my senior thesis eleven years before. Moments before the reading was to begin, I was perched nervously on the edge of a folding chair when Annie plopped herself down next to me. "I have to ask you something," she whispered, her eyes latching onto mine, her gaze so intense that I felt—as if I were nineteen again—the strongest urge to look away.

"Okay," I said, still the good student.

"Well, you and I have known each other a long time," she said. "First as student and teacher, and then, well, socially, over the years, right?"

"Right," I said, glancing at the rows of current Wesleyan students, my former professors, all these people I knew I was going to have to perform for in an instant.

"And now,"—she patted her copy of my novel as it sat in her lap—"I've read this, and I'm wondering—do you think I know you better through our actual contact or through reading your book? What do you think?"

"The novel," I said instantly. "You know me better through reading the novel. I mean, in real life we don't know each other that well. But this"—I pointed—"is like the inside of my brain."

"Yes." Annie smiled broadly. "Yes, I think that's right. Okay, get up, kiddo." She nudged me. "They're waiting. Read slowly. Knock 'em dead."

After that reading—after and before it, ever since I first read *Pilgrim at Tinker Creek*—Annie's voice, written and spoken, has stayed with me, as have the voices of all the writers I've been lucky enough to have as teachers. This is, I think, a double kind of knowing and a great privilege—to encounter writers as teachers in the classroom, and then also to go deeper, sitting, solitary, with the pages they have written—no rules, here, no checkmarks, question marks or bits of advice, just the language of their souls, the contours of their minds, the sharp, particular visions they train upon the world. Just as I told Annie that she knew me better through my work, it is in reading the writing of my teachers that I've probably learned the most from them, their voices undiluted and compressed, removed from all the static of the social world.

All these teacher-writer voices, then, live somewhere inside "Surtsey" because they live somewhere inside me. Present in perhaps more explicit ways are the voices of the various people I showed the story to in draft. Lauren, first, then Bob Chibka, my writing and teaching colleague at Boston College, who encouraged me to render Phoebe's conflicts about aloneness and connection in less familiar and more nuanced ways. Darcy Frey, who always helps me with pacing, with the mix of internal and external; Bridgette Sheridan, a historian friend who reads my work with acute psychological insight though she's never written fiction herself. My sister Ruth, her husband Michael, my husband Jim—none of them writers, all of them readers of the most discerning sort. My parents, both literary critics; my agent, Richard Parks—each of these people commented on "Surtsey" before I finally submitted it for publication, and each is thus a "mentor" to the story in some way.

There is one other person I must mention, though I've never met her and she's never read the story, and that is Canadian writer Alice Munro. Her stories read like distilled and fractured novels, brief glimpses into long and complex lives. Often I finish them with a gasp, a sense of both wonder and recognition. I might have written this, I find myself thinking, if only I were that daring, that good. I think I've tried, in "Surtsey," to give Phoebe's life a Munro-esque sense of having taken place over time, of embodying contradiction and elusiveness—of containing, that is, within a tightly controlled form, something of the spilling-over messiness of life.

Surtsey

THE INSTITUTE LOOKS LIKE it's made of Legos, or like it's an architect's model of itself. Inside, it's all shining floors and sleek Scandinavian furniture. You can't feel the elevator move. On the walls of the auditorium, chunks of rock hang. Phoebe thinks they look too rough, like a mistake. She had expected something different—dinner in a mansion in the old section of Reykjavik, a brief ceremony followed by a robust, fishy meal. Instead, the speeches were long and windy, and now frail vegetarian hors d'oeuvres are being passed around on translucent plastic trays. Her clothes feel wrong for this place, her silk sweater too patterned, her earrings too curled and elaborate, a reproduction of the jewelry in some Renaissance painting; Isaac got them for her at the Metropolitan Museum of Art.

She stands and nods—*thank you, yes thanks but of course it wasn't my work; yes, a terrible loss*—while people congratulate her, or really Isaac through her, or really Isaac. I only married him, she wants to say. At her side, her granddaughter Kirsten looks perfect in her simple black pants and gray tunic, her blunt blonde hair, her face that seems wide-open even when it's not.

Phoebe has been here before, years ago, on one of Isaac's first research trips. Then, she was twenty-six and three months pregnant with Matthew. They didn't bring Anne, who had just turned four; for some reason Phoebe no longer remembers, they left her with Isaac's parents in Boston. Each day, Phoebe would wolf down and vomit up her Icelandic breakfast: pickles and cheeses, heels of bread, rounds of hard-boiled egg, salty smoked fish. They stayed at a guest house in Reykjavik for the first days, and then Isaac went off to the Vestmann Islands to observe the volcano and Phoebe waited—sightseeing, shopping, sitting (mostly) in her room with a book, because it was January and there was no light.

One morning, a graduate student from the Institute took her in his car to the water's edge. They got out and she stood there shivering, facing south, toward Isaac. Through the dusky air, you could see columns of ash bursting forth from the eruption, rising thousands of feet into the sky. Isaac wasn't in the volcano, of course, but he was on an adjacent island, or flying above the eruption in a papery little plane, or in a boat on that metallic ocean, measuring magnetism with the other scientists on his team. Already he was an expert, getting famous, at least in certain circles. Already Phoebe's mind began to drift when he talked about his work. Later, Isaac would tell Matthew that he and the island of Surtsey had been born in the same year. Surtsey, named after a Norse fire god Surtur. When the kids were teenagers, Isaac took them on a research trip, and they got to step onto this brand-new island, which was (odd facts, she remembered) two-thirds the size of Central Park.

Isaac returned to Iceland often for as long as he could still get around by himself, sometimes staying for a week, sometimes a month. The Institute paid his airfare, gave him a room. But Phoebe never went back, until now. After Matthew had come Adam, so she'd had a lot of good excuses, but the truth was, she hadn't *liked* the place, the people too polite, the earth belching itself up in an ongoing natural disaster, its wounds unbandaged and unscabbed.

Now, though, with her own wounds just beginning to form a taut, new skin, she is back, her granddaughter beside her, the girl's thoughts unreadable beneath her ice-blue eyes. Phoebe shakes someone's hand, fiddles with her earring, feels her eyeglasses heavy on her nose. She is still trying to learn to read the world in a whole new way, to stop looking for wheelchair ramps and handicapped signs, to pack lightly and only for herself, to bring just three vials of pills: thyroid, multivitamin, estrogen replacement. Her limbs often feel floaty, as if without Isaac's chair to push, she might simply drift away. Sometimes she loves that feeling, how *loose* she is, how perfectly expendable, a wisp of smoke. At other moments, she wants to grab for Kirsten's hand— stay with me, honey, don't stray. But Kirsten is a strapping eighteen-year-old; gone is the child who used to fling herself, hair flying, into her grandmother's arms, her body one bright announcement of need.

Phoebe didn't want to come, at first. An award, fine, thank you very much, but it's not as if Isaac didn't get a roomful of them in his lifetime, and why should she cross an ocean to accept it? Who is she to them? A widow, a nobody, a wife. And to go without him, to take something meant for him—it seemed wrong somehow, or was it that she was afraid it might tip her back into the raw, impossible time right after his death a year ago? But how they pleaded, those Nordic scientists; how they managed to cajole and manipulate in their formal English: Would be so honored...such astounding contributions...not only a colleague but a dear friend. They offered her two plane tickets and she thought of Kirsten, who had dropped out of her first year of college that spring and was back home with Anne, working at a furniture store while she *found her balance*. Kirsten said yes, okay, she'd go, but not with any enthusiasm or even gratefulness. Somehow—but when?—she has turned into a sullen, withholding girl behind her lovely face, her straight, blonde hair, and blue eyes that must be from her unknown father. Anne, like Phoebe and Isaac, is small and brown-haired, or anyway Phoebe was until her hair went gray.

"Are you thirsty?" Phoebe asks, turning to Kirsten only to find that the girl is not at her side. She looks around and spots her at the high end of the auditorium. Someone is showing her things—a tall woman dressed in black, pointing to the rocks, telling her, probably, their names and properties. Phoebe doubts Kirsten is interested, but she can't be sure. Anne, after all, has turned out to be a successful scientist like her father, going back to school in her late twenties even though she was raising a child alone, Kirsten the one blip in her life, the one time she wandered from her path. Phoebe and Isaac had expected Anne to get an abortion, but she had surprised them all by giving birth at twenty-two, and it wasn't until ten years later that she got married, to an older scientist she met in the lab. After Kirsten passed through babyhood, she began to seem more like Anne's room-mate than her daughter, a top student, a gifted athlete. She could play the piano and run cross-county; she could cook. Then, this past spring, a simple announcement (*how can she,* Anne had asked Phoebe, and Phoebe thought *ah but she can*): I'm not going to school anymore, I need a break.

"And you've always lived in Massachusetts?" a woman is asking Phoebe.

"Always," she says. "Isaac, too."

How is it, she wonders, that the mouth can form phrases while the mind drifts very far away? She would like to ask the scientists to conduct an experiment on this. It interests her (she is sorry to admit) more than rocks.

"New England is a place I have never visited," the stranger is saying.

"You should come—you can stay with us!" Phoebe answers, her voice surprising her with its urgency. "With me," she corrects, then feels herself flushing, as if she has just committed some indiscretion.

"Thank you." The woman stares into her drink. "Thank you. You are kind."

BEFORE THE RECEPTION is even over, Phoebe and Kirsten are herded outside into the parking lot, taken to a car. Doors are opened. *You must be hungry; you must be tired. Please. No, after you.* The car is tiny and purple, like a toy. Phoebe tries to remember the name of the man who is driving, but the accent keeps muddling things for her and the names here all sound alike. Everyone knew Isaac. Everyone loved Isaac. People keep telling her stories—*I remember when...Once Isaac and I went....* I knew him better, she has an urge to announce as she straps herself in. She shouldn't have had wine at the reception, not with her jet lag; now she's both dizzy and tired. In her lap, she holds his award—a heavy plaque cocooned in bubble wrap. The money part of it, the check, is in her purse. As they pull away from the Institute, she lets her head fall back against the seat. Kirsten is talking, making an effort, saying something about her job. The streets now are narrower, prettier, the roofs red and blue. They go up a hill and make a sharp left turn. The driver, she notices dimly, has nice hands.

After the Institute, the restaurant is a relief. Old model ships hang from the walls next to whale harpoons; oil lamps flicker, though outside it's light as day. The man—Gunnar? Gundolf?—seats Phoebe at one end of a long plank table, Kirsten at the other end. Other people keep joining them, hello hello. Somehow, without quite meaning to, Phoebe orders another glass of wine. She never drank much when Isaac was alive—his health was too fragile and she didn't want to tempt him—but now she has wine almost every night. The man who drove the car sits to her left. To her right is a woman around Phoebe's age, perhaps his wife. Phoebe feels, as she sits there, oddly calm and happy, like a child watching an adult dinner party without having to join in herself. At first she isn't sure why, then she realizes—they're speaking Icelandic; they have forgotten, for a moment, to be hosts.

Before long, though, the man who drove the car turns to her. "You will try a native dish?"

"Yes," says Phoebe, hoping she can stomach it. "If you'll order for me. If you don't mind."

Questions, he asks her, then, as the table fills with food. About the occupations of her children, the scandal with the President, New

England architecture. He knows her children's names, all of them; he met them, he says, when Isaac brought them to see Surtsey. Ad-dam, he says. Ad-dam, Matthew, Awn. Phoebe drinks her wine and eats the mysterious, rubbery food without asking what it is. He brings up poetry, says he likes Emily Dickinson and Walt Whitman. She realizes she cannot name a single Icelandic writer, not one, though she knows from the guidebook that this is one of the most literate countries in the world. As she searches for something informed to say, a young woman leans across the table.

"And you do...?" she asks, her accent thick.

"Do?" Phoebe repeats.

"For, ah..., you know, *vork*," says the woman. "For a *jub*."

"I...I raised my children," Phoebe stumbles. "And I did some writing for a newsletter before Isaac got...." Her voice snags. She reaches for her wine.

"She has an extraordinary garden, filled with rare specimens," says the man beside her, and then it is as if she is falling, tumbling back in time, for this, this could be Isaac, this could be Phoebe and Isaac at some other award dinner, in Ann Arbor or Ithaca or Chicago. Somebody asks her what she does and Isaac jumps in and saves her: her extraordinary garden, pulmonaria and petunias, clematis and digitalis, yes she knows the Latin names, and meanwhile Isaac is dropping his fork, is trying to cut his meat with hands that no longer work, but she *lets him be*, she does not reach across to cut his meat as if he were a child.

"How do you know about my garden?" she asks now.

"It's world famous," the man says.

"No it's not, I don't even do it anymore, I—" It takes her a second to realize he's joking. His smile is wry and charming, his eyes gleam. The woman who asked the question has turned toward Kirsten, who is holding court at the other end of the table, more animated than Phoebe has seen her in months.

"You don't remember me, do you?" asks the man.

Phoebe, chewing, nods, though she does not.

"I'm Gunnar Gunnarson," he says, and again the air in the room shifts and Phoebe draws her legs in, thinking no, I do, of course I do, because suddenly she does: He must be the one who took her to the water's edge, the graduate student assigned to drive her around, and then it's as if she's looking at one of her own sons grown swiftly old, his features coarsened, his shoulders wider, his hair, like hers, gone gray. She tries to remember what he used to look like and can't, though her stomach is fluttering with something she can't quite grasp.

"You told me then about your garden," he says. "And Isaac told me, too, many times. I was...sometimes I was a little jealous." He pauses, raises his eyebrows. "We can't grow gardens like that here."

"*No*," she says, and the word comes out too forcefully. His hand lifts his fork, the easy gesture of a man whose body works. She pictures Isaac next to her and feels a painful spasm—of grief, or perhaps desire.

"Do you have children?" she asks, seeking safer ground.

He nods. "A daughter, Sigrid. She's eighteen, like your Kirsten."

"Kirsten's my granddaughter."

"I know," he says. "I married late, and for a short time."

He is leaning toward her. Underneath the table, she feels heat radiating off his leg. She sees the stubble of his beard, the dark tunnels of his nostrils, the laugh-lines around his eyes. He is, she realizes, a charmer, what her mother would have called a lady's man. Is he? His tie is purple, his shirt deep blue. He is making the moves on her. Is he? How extraordinary. He remembers her garden, he was friends with her husband. A memory begins to rise in her—the thickness of a coat, the broad whiteness of a hand—but she swallows it with another bite of this food she cannot name. Mingle, she tells herself. Mix and mingle. She takes a breath and asks a question of the person on her right.

AS THEY WALK TO THE CAR, he asks her: Dinner, the day after tomorrow, would she like to? Maybe Kirsten could go out with Sigrid, he says. With Sigrid and her friends.

Phoebe turns to look for Kirsten, who is lagging behind. Tomorrow is their day for sightseeing alone. The next day, they're to go to a museum with some of the scientists. The day after that, home. "Maybe," she says, then realizes how rude she sounds. "I mean, thank you, I'd like to, I'm just not—"

"Only if you'd really like to," he says. "Or all four of us, Kirsten and Sigrid, too."

"Yes, I'll talk to her, I'll—" They have reached the car. It's so light out; it keeps surprising her. "Thank you," she repeats.

"No," says Gunnar. "I..." His voice catches.

Don't, she thinks. *Isaac*, she thinks, and wants to weep.

Then he is opening the car door, ushering them inside, driving them to the guest house, bidding them good-night. He shakes Kirsten's hand, then hers. His hand is dry and broad and warm.

"Thank you," Phoebe blurts out for the third time. "The award would mean a lot to Isaac."

"I miss him very much," Gunnar says quietly. "Seeing you is like seeing him. And—" He lets go of her hand. "Like seeing you. Good-night."

It is not until an hour later, as she lies starkly awake in bed, that she remembers the award, left on the seat of his car.

THE NEXT DAY, PHOEBE AND KIRSTEN take the car the Institute has rented for them to a hot springs called the Blue Lagoon. At first, as they pull up, they think they have lost their way and stumbled upon a factory, huge silver smokestacks spewing forth white plumes of smoke into the overcast sky. It turns out that a geothermal power plant has been built on the site to harness the energy of the hot springs. Crouched at its foot is a low building, a blue sign, a waving, antic set of flags. A tour bus pulls up, and people in rain gear get out. Kirsten lunges forward to buy tickets before the crush.

Inside, the dressing room is filled with girls and women changing in and out of bathing suits. Phoebe looks for a private stall but there are none. Reluctantly, she takes off her slacks, begins to unbutton her blouse. Kirsten's body as she undresses is startling—the full breasts of a woman, hips wider than you'd think. Phoebe turns toward the wall and strips, feeling her granddaughter's eyes on her. Her bathing suit is old, stretched out. A sturdy blonde child darts by her, reminding her of Kirsten as a little girl. Two naked women stand chatting in Icelandic. One scratches her neck as she speaks; the other rubs lotion on her arm. Old, Phoebe thinks, admiring their ease at the same time that she notices their wrinkles, their short-cropped, practical hair. Of course they must be around her age.

Outside, the air smells of sulfur; she tastes it, rotten egg, beneath her tongue. It's drizzling, the sky pale gray. In the fog and without her glasses, she sees the scene as if it were a dream—the laden air, the bathers moving in and out of focus, and behind them, the enormous silver smokestacks belching steam. She steps into the water, feeling its sting, its heat. Wait, she means to say to Kirsten, but already the girl has disappeared into the mist. Phoebe keeps her hand along the edge of the pool, then lets go and walks deeper until water laps the bottoms of her breasts. A man brushes by her, muttering in another language. There must be a tour group of Americans here; English words keep coming to her, disembodied: *awesome, camera, shampoo.*

She stands in the water and tips her head back. The clouds of steam cascading from the smokestacks remind her of something—a natural disaster, a vision of the future or past apocalypse, Hiroshima or Auschwitz, and she wants Kirsten safely at her side. But no, of course not, this is clean power, that's all—nature harnessed into energy—and then her vision shifts and she sees the plumes as if in the negative of a photograph: the whites black, the blacks white, the images reversed. It's Surtsey, of course, that she sees, re-sees. It's Surtsey, Isaac's baby, why he came here in the first place, why he's getting, or she's getting for him, an award. The volcano looked like this when she saw it from the shore—like this but larger, black where this is white.

And then, almost despite herself, it surfaces—the memory she's been dodging, the image waiting just under the surface of her skin: She had *vomited* when she first saw Surtsey, right in front of the graduate student Gunnar, who was acting as her guide. She had seen the spewing and thought of Isaac out there somewhere and pictured Anne in New York, feverish with wailing or (which was worse?) indifferent to her absence, and she'd felt a rising, ducked her head, and vomited in one shameful, bitter spurt.

To save face, she had told Gunnar her secret, that she was expecting a baby though she wasn't showing yet. And he said oh oh, he blushed and produced a shabby handkerchief for her to use to wipe her mouth. He said a baby, how nice, how good for you, how lucky. In there, he said, pointing to her coat, his voice as full of wonder as if he had just, at that very moment, learned about the miracle of human life.

Then (the memory floats through the steam, through the thick egg smell) he touched her (did he?). He put his hand flat across her belly, over her coat, while she held her breath because she knew she stank of vomit, and because suddenly desire was rattling through her like a cough. She didn't tell him about Anne, didn't say I have a child already, we left her back home, a girl who just turned four. I should go back, she said—something like that—and he made a noise inside his throat, a moan, a strangled word. Yes, he said, then. Yes, of course, and if her breath hadn't been sour, she would have kissed him, a chaste kiss, a wet, loose, hungry kiss, hot tongue, cold air, Isaac in a boat, Anne left like an orphan in New York. She had left them, they had left her. Soon there would be another baby; her life would settle deeper into its groove. Gunnar placed his gloved hand over her cheek, and she tipped her face into his hand and let it rest there for a second, and then she said it again: *I should go back.*

That afternoon at the guest house, she had touched herself guiltily, thoughts of Isaac slipping moistly into thoughts of Gunnar, their arms, their legs, their blended, milky sperm. She had wanted them both, at the same time that she had wanted neither one of them, to keep her body hers. Once, years later, she had a real affair, brief and depressing, with the father of one of Adam's classmates. It went on for two weeks while Isaac was in Iceland with the kids. Afterward, she told him about it. At first he was angry, but not as angry as she thought he should be—as she had perhaps *wanted* him to be. Then he forgave her and for a while their own lovemaking grew urgent and exciting, and then Isaac got sick and she knew she could never again betray him, not when his own body was doing so, one muscle at a time.

Now she feels a hand on her arm and startles.

"It's me, Nana." Kirsten thrusts her face through the steam. "Isn't this weird? It gets hotter and hotter. Over there, it's practically boiling."

Kirsten is bright pink, her wet hair plastered to her head. Phoebe herself is beginning to feel lightheaded, almost drunk.

"Did you do the clay?" asks Kirsten.

"What?"

"The clay. Over there." She points into the vapor. "People rub it on their bodies—I guess it's good for your skin or something. Come see."

Slowly, then, as if she's moving through a medium thicker than water, Phoebe follows her granddaughter until they come to a corner filled with people bending into the muck, grabbing handfuls of mud and smearing it over their torsos, arms and legs. Phoebe is confused;

she thought the pool was man-made, with concrete edges, but now she isn't sure. She recoils—dank mud, pale bodies, a breeding ground for germs—but beside her Kirsten keeps saying things like *healing, soothing*, so finally Phoebe scoops up a fistful of gunk (Isaac would have known the proper term) and dribbles it halfheartedly along one arm.

Then Kirsten is speaking close to her ear. *Turn around,* she says, *turn around,* so Phoebe does, and Kirsten starts to coat her back with the stuff, one handful and then another while Phoebe stands obedient, stiff at first, then slowly relaxing into her granddaughter's sure touch. Girl of her girl, daughter of her daughter, this Kirsten, smoothing her down like she's a clay sculpture or a child, and for an instant, the distance between them closes and Phoebe thinks I love you but says only *thanks Kirsty, that feels nice,* and her words wreck the moment because Kirsten takes her hand away and turns. Okay, now, you do me.

THE NIGHT, THEY HAVE AN EARLY DINNER in a restaurant Kirsten read about in the guidebook. Phoebe gets blackbird in currant sauce like in the nursery rhyme, the bird so tiny that it seems almost cruel to eat it, with its arched brown back and toothpick bones. Her hair feels coarse and ruined, like horsehair—it must be from something in the water—but her skin, lungs, and mind feel buoyant and elastic, clean. After a cup of decaf, she is ready to return to the guest house, but Kirsten wants to explore. For the first time, Phoebe lets her drive the car; bit by bit, Kirsten is taking over the logistics of the trip.

"You're much less bossy than my mother," Kirsten tells her happily. "I'm an excellent driver. You'll see."

It seems only a matter of moments before they are out of the city, driving north into a landscape so bare, so treeless and unpopulated, that the road itself looks out of place. The ground keeps changing color; sometimes it's black, sometimes a grayish green, as if covered by a sort of Spanish moss.

"Let's get out," Phoebe says suddenly. "Let's take a little walk," so Kirsten pulls over and they step onto the spongy turf. Phoebe bends down. What grows here? *Something* must grow here, alpine flowers, maybe. Hardy, wind-resistant plants.

Kirsten plucks a piece of dry, rough foliage. "What is that?"

Phoebe takes it; it is papery dry but surprisingly tough. "I don't know."

"But you're the gardener."

"I'm not." She tries to make her voice less sharp. "Anyway," she says, "this is different from what grows at home. Grandpa would know, but I don't."

"He came here a lot, didn't he? They all know him."

Phoebe nods. They have started walking. She looks behind her to make sure they don't lose sight of the car. The ground is bumpy, full of dips and humps. She half-wants to take Kirsten's arm, but she's too afraid the girl might stiffen or step away.

"Did you mind?" Kirsten asks. "I mean, that he came here so much? That he worked so hard and traveled all the time?"

"It mattered to him," says Phoebe. "He didn't see it as work, exactly."

"Except then he got sick," Kirsten says. "I mean, he could've had more fun if he'd known it was going to happen. He could've taken more real vacations or—I don't know—spent more time with his family. All that work didn't even matter in the end."

"Of course it mattered." Phoebe feels a fierce need to defend Isaac, even as part of her agrees. "He made extremely important contributions—you heard those people yesterday. But also it...he loved his work, his work *saved* him—"

The words surprise her. People tell her she saved him, but when she hears herself saying otherwise, she knows she is right. He loved her, of course he did, but not like he loved the earth, his instruments of measure, his long-term studies, exhaustive lists. She had started out as one of his students; it was such a cliché. Isaac's class fulfilled her college science requirement. It wasn't easy for her, all those formulas; she had needed extra help. She was intent and busy, serious, not the dating sort, but also pretty—or so she was told—in a brown-eyed, birdlike way. Men came after her, even when—especially when—she wore her indifference like a cloak. In her English and French classes, she was an excellent student. One professor encouraged her to get a doctorate. Isaac didn't tell her not to apply to graduate school or go for her teaching certificate, didn't say why don't you drop it all and have a baby, but somehow it had happened like that, her energy transferred, suddenly, from the lit library late at night to rice cereal on the stove, diapers in the wash. And she had loved her babies—their skin, their sounds, the way they slept through sirens and woke with reaching arms. She had loved Isaac, too, hadn't she? Her older man, her scientist: his craggy energy, his cataloguing mind, the way he seemed to watch her gently, from afar. She keeps one of his lists in her wallet, still, cut from a postcard he sent her from Surtsey in 1967:

> 16 species of algae
> 4 species of vascular plants on beach (floaters)
> 2 species of moss (anemochores)
> 12 species of marine invertebrate in tide pools
> 26 species of insects
> 1 species of spider
> gulls inland, nesting in hills & cliffs, Love, I.

When—rarely—she looks at it, she feels a daunting mix of tenderness and rage.

"That man Gunnar Gunnarson asked me to have dinner with him tomorrow," she tells Kirsten.

"You're kidding." Kirsten wrinkles her nose. "Really? Alone?"

Phoebe shrugs. "He has a daughter around your age; he thought you might like to meet her. I guess his daughter is going out with a few friends or something." She sighs. "I don't know."

"What," says Kirsten. "You mean you're going to start dating an Icelandic guy? You'd move to Iceland, Nana? At your age? You'd just—"

"Dinner," Phoebe interrupts gently, but the words are bouncing around inside her head: "dating," "guy," "move," "age." She's only sixty-two, too young to have an eighteen-year-old granddaughter. She stops and prods the ground with her foot. "Don't be ridiculous, Kirsten. I'm not moving anywhere."

"But you want to have dinner with him."

"No," she says, and suddenly, inexplicably, her eyes fill with tears.

"I think you should," says Kirsten. "We're on vacation. You should go."

"It might be nice for you to meet his daughter."

"Whatever. Or I'll do something else."

"Like what?"

"Like . . . walk around or sit in a café. Or have a baby. There are tons of single mothers here—I read about it. It's totally accepted. The government helps support them."

Phoebe shakes her head. "You're much too young to have a baby. You have a whole life to lead."

"Shop, then. For my mom's birthday present. It's in two weeks, you know."

"You can't shop at night."

"Things stay open here. People start partying at one A.M."

"You have a whole life to lead," repeats Phoebe. "Don't be in any rush to have a baby."

"*Stop it*," Kirsten bursts out, her voice grinding.

Phoebe takes a step back and looks at her.

"It's like you want me to know *everything*," says Kirsten. "You want me to see the whole thing like it's already happened, but I can't, I won't, and anyway I'm not you and I'm not my mother. You know, some people actually want to have children—"

"Don't be ridiculous. Your mother wanted children and so did I, desperately, more than anything, it's just... it's just I also wanted—"

What had she also wanted? She can't remember now, or maybe it wasn't clear enough even then. To be alone, perhaps, as self-sufficient as a solitary fish, weaving in and out of light, of darkness, changing direction with a swerve of torso, flick of tail. Or no—to be more in the world, among its people, to do something with all her thoughts, for she had so many, every day, every second. Everybody did, of course, but so did she. She had wanted (was that it?) something solid and enduring that wouldn't twist and shudder, wouldn't deflate like an old beach ball and one day cease—how impossible—to be. Not to be a scientist, though, not like her daughter, her husband, and one of her sons. As the kids got older, she had taken courses in literature, written some poems and a few articles for the newsletter put out by the local historical society. Her garden was—everyone said so—a work of art, and filled with rocks from around the world. She had been on the brink of something, then, her job as a mother essentially finished, her children successful, Anne getting her doctorate, Matthew in medical school, Adam working at the UN.

But then Isaac got sick and the house, emptied of children, filled up with walkers and wheelchairs, metal bars, sheepskin pads. The garden grew clogged. She helped her husband. In sickness and in health. She answered his letters, typed his ideas, changed his diapers. Toward the end, they had a nurse come in for night shifts. Isaac hated that. He barked at the nurse; he turned tyrannical and childish. He wanted only, he told Phoebe, to be able to feed himself, crap into a toilet, and do his work. His face grew rocky like the earth he studied, molten lava hardened into stone. The nurse quit and Phoebe didn't hire another. I'm sorry, he told her once when she had bronchitis but still got up for him in the middle of the night. Just once, he said it—*I'm sorry, love, for all of it*—but it was enough. He would have done the same for her. She wasn't angry except lately, now and then, in sudden, odd bursts that flatten her. Egotist, she finds herself thinking. Sexist, self-serving, self-important, dead fool. But no, surely it is the illness that deserves her rage.

Kirsten is walking away from her, stepping confidently over the ground that seems to Phoebe so treacherous, holes springing up out of nowhere, cracks where the earth has split. She should know the scientific names for things like "earth," "crack," and "split." She has, after all, typed Isaac's work and sat in the audience while he gave lectures. Now the words return to her, more sound than meaning: *Faultscarp, tephra, alkali-olivine basalt, pahoe-hoe lava, phenocrysts.*

"Where are you going?" she calls to Kirsten, her own voice seeming quavery to her, lost in so much space.

Kirsten turns. "Sweden," she says. "I want to find out why Grandpa never got the Nobel Prize." But then she tosses her head and starts back.

"I just want the best for you," Phoebe tells her when they're standing side by side. "I don't mean to lecture you. You'll find your way. Of course you will."

Kirsten tosses her head. "I'm not going to grad school like my parents. I might not even finish college. This family thinks there's only one way to do things, but the world"—she gestures at it, moonlike and unpeopled—"does things in a thousand different ways."

"Yes," says Phoebe, remembering Anne at Kirsten's age, how focused she was. When Anne was in graduate school, Isaac could still walk. Phoebe used to stay home with Kirsten while he and Anne circled the reservoir near the house, discussing—what?—rocks and atoms, plants and algae, she supposes, but then why did she always feel so left out? The boys had been more open with her, less withheld, but they, too, seemed to see her as a pale figure on the margins, always present and thus easy to forget. Or is it—has it always been—her own anxieties that place her there? Suddenly she sees, as if in a pile on the ground, all the gifts her children and husband have given her over the years: vases and jewelry boxes, blank books, birdfeeders, a silk eye pillow filled with lavender, the cashmere scarf twined, right now, around her neck. And less material gifts: What are you thinking about, Mom? I can hire someone to type them, Pheebes. They were good to her, so why does she sometimes feel so sour, curdled, *tricked*? Nobody warned her. Nobody said *make sure to find a chip of rock, a steel nugget or chunk of coal—something solid and inhuman to clench in your mouth when the human world spins far away.*

"What'll you wear on your date?" Kirsten asks.

"Oh stop, Kirsty. It's not a date."

"Of course it is," says Kirsten. "I can lend you earrings." She pauses. "I hope you brought birth control. Don't be in any rush to have a baby."

The laugh comes up in Phoebe almost like a shudder, then turns into a bright bubble, rises, and pops. She hugs her tall granddaughter, holds her close, breathing in her half-child, half-grown-woman smell. Kirsten cups her hand on the back of Phoebe's head the way a man would except that with Isaac, for the past ten years, it was always she who was bending down toward him.

"We should get back," she says, pulling away.

"Why?" asks Kirsten. "It's light forever. It's only nine o'clock."

They get in the car, then, but instead of turning around on the narrow road, Kirsten drives farther north, up toward the rocky cliffs in the distance, over a bridge that spans a rushing stream. They pass a few houses huddled together, a squat barn, a gash where steam rises from the earth. They drive on and on, and then they are in a place where there are no houses, only rocks, dark and tumbled, and here and there a small sign directing them to destinations they have never heard of: Pingvellir, Hvolsvollur.

"The astronauts use this as their training ground because it's the closest thing to the moon," Kirsten says at one point, and Phoebe thinks yes, of course.

THEY DRIVE AND DRIVE through the clear northern light, and she sees Isaac in the rocky passes, Isaac in the long pipes bringing steam heat from the hot springs to the people, Isaac in the horses who turn to look as they pass by. She sees him clearly and everywhere and yet from very far away, as if he is in another country, on another planet, a place of hard scientific truths or bits of poetry—it was, with him, never entirely clear. She always half-suspected that he had a lover here, a woman he saw on his research trips, but now she sees it wasn't so. The land itself was what he came for: the frozen lava fields, the hidden plants struggling to grow, the water issued from the center of the earth.

Her blue blouse, she would wear, if she could have dinner with Isaac now. A gauzy scarf of Kirsten's, who winds it twice around her head. At this dinner, Isaac's body is whole. He is here at the source, at this place that, though it feels so old, is still the youngest landscape in the world. And she? She is young and full of something—a narrow, bright desire, a sharp ambition: *I'll do this, I'll go here, I'll make this, find that.* They might have been partners, co-travelers, if only she had been more open, forced herself closer to the edge. She never told him how lost she sometimes felt. He knew—of course he did—but oh how tactful they were, how gentle and circumspect. *Have you seen Phoebe's garden? You should take a look.* And never did she say don't go when it was time for another trip, and never did she say *I'll come,* though the ache in those early days was like another baby in her belly, kicking cruelly at her gut.

Or not Isaac but another. Gunnar Gunnarson. One of the Gunnars—half the men in Iceland have the same name. A date. Her first in over forty years. He remembered that she loved gardening. He'll take her to dinner. She'll eat something she's never eaten before, puffin, perhaps, or shark. Maybe afterward she'll go home with him, feel him against her, inside her. She'll never see him again but it doesn't matter. You could turn into nothing in a place like this, a splinter of rock, a puff of steam. You could turn into nothing or find that your heart is pumping hard, your muscles stretching long, your body still carrying you across the world.

"Let's go back," Phoebe says, suddenly tired, and Kirsten nods but keeps driving.

"It's late," says Phoebe. Her watch reads eleven-forty-five.

Kirsten squints at the horizon. "It's so light. How do they sleep? How do they stop—" Then she stops herself, as if she's said something wrong. "I'm sorry, Nana. Should I turn around? Do you want to go back?"

Phoebe switches on the car radio. The language is hard and edgy, guttural. For a moment she thinks she understands something, then the words slide out of reach. It never gets dark here, not until winter, when it never gets light. Her whole body is aching, is wanting, like a memory, or maybe in a whole new way. "No," she says. "Go on."

Sylvia A. Watanabe

SYLVIA A. WATANABE teaches at Oberlin College. Her
short fiction has received an O. Henry award, and her
nonfiction has appeared in the Pushcart Prize
anthology. She is the author of *Talking To the Dead and
Other Stories* published by Doubleday.

Looking

>>>>>>>>>>>>>>>>>>>>×<<<<<<<<<<<<<<<<<<<

An airy room, all white and yellow; everything in its place—the shine on the kettle, the potted plants on the sill, the pretty white dishes gleaming through glass cupboard doors. On the table in the breakfast nook, tidy stacks of books and sheets of manuscript covered with meticulous notes. Next to these a large metal contraption, equipped with a bookstand, an electric bulb, and a powerful ten-inch magnifying glass, like an enormous eye.

Shortly after retiring from teaching, Dorothy explained, she had begun having trouble with her sight. It was as if a hole had been burned into the center of her field of vision—a pinpoint, at first, that kept widening and widening, swallowing up bits of landscape, people's faces, the stairs on the rickety wooden staircase leading down to her house, the words on a page. It was the words she minded losing most. An opthalmologist eventually diagnosed her trouble as macular degeneration. She gave me a tour of the contraption in the breakfast nook, demonstrating how it worked—here's where you mounted the text and how you positioned the magnifying glass—not exactly something you could put in your pocket and take on the bus, she said, but it kept her reading. She was too busy now to go blind, she added, gesturing toward the stacks of books, the manuscript she was editing.

It was Dorothy Vella who taught me that writing was seeing. She was the first of my real writing teachers, and even now as I try to describe what this meant, I turn to the task with eyes she has trained.

I enrolled in her nonfiction workshop during my last term as an undergraduate at the University of Hawaii. No student was late on the first day of class. The chairs in the back of the room were filled with hopeful wait-listers. Five, then ten minutes went by, and a young woman walked in—skirts swinging, bracelets jangling on her wrists. She was wearing white pumps and hosiery with a run in it, on the back of her left leg. Without looking around, she walked straight to the chalkboard, picked up a piece of chalk, and wrote English 480: Restoration Drama in big, sprawly letters. The room rustled, as students paged through course schedules. Someone up front raised his hand. Excuse me, he said, have they changed the room for Advanced Nonfiction? The woman turned, her gaze moving from face to face. As she hurried away, Dorothy strode in, an imposing figure with shaggy white hair and a sheaf of papers under one arm. Her first instructions: Write what you *saw*.

When she had finished, she had us examine what we had written. We looked at the words that we had used: pretty, shy, bewildered, professor, fashionable, embarrassed; she asked us to pick out the judgments, invisible to us at first, that swept observation aside, substituting their own emotional burden. Turn that lens away from your navel, she said. Learn to train that camera *outward*.

Over the coming weeks, she built upon this elementary lesson, as she guided us through exercises in point of view, tonal effects, the uses of omission and indirection. First the seeing, then the telling. From one assignment to the next, we struggled to turn our attention outward, then to find the language for what we saw. It was a careful, additive process, which Dorothy likened to hand-building in clay. A process of embodiment, adding detail to detail, building a mood, a time and place, a world. Crack those abstractions open, she told us, the airy nothings: Love, Justice, Goodness, Sorrow. Look at what's inside—the smell of the weather, the shape of the light, the way a character crosses a room or holds her cup as she sips her tea.

Look, Dorothy instructed. Just look.

After a number of lessons focusing on what we saw and knew, she gave us an exercise in narrating what we couldn't see and had no way of remembering. Our assignment was to interview someone who had been living in Hawaii during the attack on Pearl Harbor (the members of our class too young to have experienced this) and then, out of the interview, to construct a narrative, as fully embodied as if we'd been there. I chose to talk with my father and two of my uncles. I carefully wrote out a list of questions, then set up appointments, at which, armed with a tape recorder, I covered the same ground over and over, seeking what happened, what came first, where things were, who was there. But memory faltered, accounts varied, and I found myself filling in the blanks from my own imagination. When I turned the assignment in, I felt I had done something dangerous: I had written fiction. I explained this to Dorothy, who laughed. "I suppose I have taught you something, then."

It is no exaggeration, now, over fifteen years later, to say that everything I write shows her influence. "Where People Know Me," the story included in this collection, perhaps most closely follows the shape of her instruction because it is built on the boundary between fiction and nonfiction; because it has set itself the task of writing strong emotion by only indirectly naming it; and because, more than anything else, it is about seeing when I wanted so badly to look away.

Where People Know Me

LATE AT NIGHT, long after the other residents in the senior care facility have gone to sleep, Big Grandma is wakeful. She whirs down the fourth floor hall in her electric wheelchair, past the nurses' station where the RN on duty is bent over a stack of medical records, and stops in front of the elevator. By the time security catches up with her, she is on the ground floor, headed out the lobby toward the parking lot. When they ask where she is going, she answers in Japanese, "Where people know me."

This is what the night nurse reports to my mother's oldest sister, Tee, who tells Mother, who calls long distance from Honolulu to tell me. Meanwhile, Aunt Tee has gotten in touch with Aunt Esther, the second oldest. Esther is offended at not being notified before my mother, even though Esther hasn't spoken to Big Grandma in years. Esther then gets back to Tee's daughter, who tells her mother, who phones my mother again and claims the whole thing is making it so she can't sleep nights. "You're the one who went to college," Aunt Tee says. "Why is Mama doing this to me?"

HERE IN WYOMING, MICHIGAN, we've been having a week of record cold when Mother's call comes. The day's high was ten degrees, and the mercury's dropping as darkness falls. "You probably don't get many attempted escapes from the Senior Home there," she observes.

It's been more than ten years since my husband's search for a college teaching position took us away from the Islands; for the last four, we've lived in Michigan. During this whole time, between occasional visits, Mother and I have kept in touch several times a week by telephone. Recently I began my own business, freelancing from home as a technical writer, and she worries that I do not get out enough.

"There are too many hermits in this family," she says, right after telling me about the furor over my grandmother.

"Hermits? In *this* family?" I do not try to conceal my disbelief.

Today Dad has gone to a meeting of his retirees union, and she has the house to herself. "Days of Our Lives" is playing on the television in the background. After the family news, she gives me the rundown on her Birthday Girls Lunch Club, her arthritis exercise group, and her General Electric cooking class. The cooking class, which has adopted the motto "Encounter the good tastes of American cuisine," has moved on from ethnic desserts to ethnic salads. I am relieved to hear this since my waistline cannot tolerate many more encounters with the good tastes of Turkish baklava or Hungarian chocolate rum torte, which have been arriving with regularity by two-day priority mail.

It is hard to believe, laughing with her, that not long ago she had cancer surgery. But the doctors found the tumor early, and after a few months of recuperation, Mother has resumed her full social calendar. "It's like calling the sickness back to keep talking about it," she finally tells me, exasperated with being cross-examined about her latest medical checkup.

Now, before going off to prepare one of of her ethnic desserts for a housewarming party, she fills me in on the neighborhood gossip. The Kanaheles' divorced son has moved back in with them. The Satos are traveling in India. The ugly Labrador retriever puppy next door has turned out to be a rottweiler. "I realize you're very busy…," she segues, and I know that someone will require birthday greetings, congratulations, or get-well wishes that she knows I will probably fail to send.

After we hang up, I sit in my darkening kitchen and watch the lights come on in the surrounding houses. It occurs to me that it's been days since I've seen any of the people who live in them.

The next time we talk, I tell her, "It's just that everyone around here keeps to themselves. Not like it is back home with everybody in each other's business. I can't hear myself think when I'm at home."

"I bet you get a lot of thinking done there." Her reply is without irony. "What do you think about?"

I can't help laughing then. "Oh, about what it's like back home."

MY NEXT VISIT TO THE ISLANDS is in April, a few months after Big Grandma's near-escape. It's been a whole year since the last time I was back, when Mother was in the hospital. As soon as we arrive home from the airport, she starts reminding me to call people. "Don't forget to get in touch with Aunt Tee," she says. "And Aunt Esther—you know how she is. And your dad's sister Winnie has been phoning every day for a week...."

It is late afternoon, and the humidity suddenly seems stifling. I go to the telephone and dial. When my husband, Hal, answers, there is an echo on the line. "Hello-hello." His voice fades in and out. "It's snowing—snowing—here...."

THE FOLLOWING MORNING, Mother and I drop by Esther's on our way to pick up Aunt Tee, who is going with us to visit Big Grandma. After her husband died a few years ago, Aunt Esther developed a fear of prowlers. She keeps all her windows fastened and her curtains drawn, even during the day. From the outside, it is impossible to tell that anyone is home, but Mother assures me that Esther hardly ever ventures out, unless accompanied either by herself or Tee. Aunt Esther has also had a locksmith install a dead bolt and a couple of additional locks on the living room door, and we can hear her undoing these as we stand on the front stoop, in the drizzle, with our cardboard boxes of homemade food.

After she lets us in, she disappears into the kitchen with the boxes, while we make our way through the stacks of newspapers and magazines

Sylvia A. Watanabe »»«« 159

lining the dim foyer, to the cluttered living room. A reading lamp glows on the end table next to the couch and a game show is playing on TV.

"Oh, 'Hollywood Squares,'" Mother says. "I watch that sometimes."

"I never do. I just keep the sound on for the company." Aunt Esther has materialized in the doorway. Her gaunt face is framed by stiff gray curls, and she is wearing a pants outfit of bluish gray.

When we leave, we invite her to come with us, but she declines, as she always does. "You were the favorite," she tells my mother. "Mama would never know that I was there."

THE SENIOR CARE FACILITY occupies an entire wing of the medical center where Mother had her cancer operation the year before. As she, Aunt Tee, and I step out of the elevator, my aunt explains that the night staff have tried using medication, even physical restraint, to curtail Big Grandma's nocturnal wandering. But she has not let up on her determined resistance, which now includes occasional episodes of biting. "They have confiscated her dentures," Aunt Tee says, barely able to contain her mortification. If you bring any edibles for Big Grandma, you must go to the nurses' station and ask for her teeth. My aunt stops there to do so, and also to drop off the loaves of mango bread she has baked that morning. "Penance food," my mother whispers, as Aunt Tee distributes mango bread and expresses our thanks and apologies all around.

Big Grandma is sitting up in bed, dozing or pretending to doze, when we arrive at her room. Someone has dressed her in a baby-blue duster, trimmed with lace, and braided her white hair with pink and yellow ribbons. It is a new look for my ninety-six-year-old grandmother.

"Isn't that nice?" Aunt Tee says too brightly.

"Easter-egg colors," my mother adds. They both have the same fixed smile on their faces—the same smile, I suddenly realize, that is on mine. As we stand grimacing at Big Grandma, I resist the impulse to reach over and pull the ribbons from her hair.

She opens her eyes and lies back on the pillows, looking us over. Seeing that she has awakened, Mother gestures at me to approach, then says, "Look, look who's come to see you all the way from Michigan."

Big Grandma regards me blankly.

"It's Aya," my mother says. "From Michigan."

"Where?" Big Grandma asks, turning her good ear toward us.

"Mee-shee-gen," Mother repeats, louder.

"Ah," Big Grandma replies. She glances around the room, then back at me, comprehension dawning on her face. "I was wondering where this was."

IN MY MEMORY, she is always dressed in dark colors, muted pin stripes and floral prints. She wears black tabis and straw slippers on her feet. Her hair is neatly oiled and pulled away from her face into a knot that is held in place with brown plastic combs. My grandmother seems always to have thought of herself as old. "You can't be free until you're old," she told me once. Though widowed young, she was never tempted to remarry. "I'd already had one husband," she said. "I didn't need another."

It seemed curious that she should speak of freedom with such spirit when she had more rules than anyone I ever knew. She had rules for what colors and styles to wear, rules for the order in which family members took a bath or got served dinner, and rules for eating at table (take less than your fill, never leave a single grain of rice in your bowl, refuse the last piece of chicken). The whole time she was living with Aunt Tee, for as far back as anyone could remember, the entire household was run by Big Grandma's rules.

There is a right way and a wrong way, according to Big Grandma. This is the right way to address an elder. This is how you speak to someone younger. This is how you sit. This is how you hold a cup. This is how you hand an object to another person. When I was six or seven, she instructed me in the proper use of chopsticks. After demonstrating how to hold them (thumb on the bottom, middle finger between, index finger on top), she handed me the pair and a bowl of Rice Krispies, then told me to pick out the grains of cereal, one by one.

My mother and her sisters also went through this training. "You had it easy," Aunt Tee assures me. "The only teaching aid she used with us was the flat side of a wooden cooking spoon."

After their father died and Big Grandma went to work as a live-in housekeeper for a wealthy family, she was away from home for days at a time. This left Aunt Tee, who was just twelve, at the head of a household of little girls.

"When you think about it, we could have gone wild," my mother says.

Then Aunt Tee adds, "If I hadn't made you stick to the rules."

<hr/>

STILL, THERE IS ANOTHER SIDE to my grandmother they never mention—a side familiar to me from the hours, days, and months spent in her company. Each weekday morning, till I was old enough to go to school, my mother dropped me off at Tee's on her way to work. When I arrived, Big Grandma was already puttering in the garden. I sat under a big mango tree while she brought me fresh fruit to go with my milk and toast. Sometimes there were fresh litchis or pomegranates. "This is what silkworms eat," she said offering me a handful of purple mulberries. In mango season, when it was time to harvest the bright red and golden fruit, I helped to spot them among the shady branches and we picked mangoes until she had a fragrant apronful.

Sometimes in the afternoon, we went for a bus ride to the sweet shop and the dry goods store downtown. More often, though, we visited the sundry healers and prayer ladies in her acquaintance—including a clairvoyant herbalist and an acupuncturist nun—whose treatments eased the symptoms of her arthritis. She herself claimed the ability to heal with the energy flowing from her hands, and I can still see her, sitting up late into the night beside my sickbed, the touch of her cool palms upon my skin, while her lips move silently, chanting prayers.

WHEN I ASK MY MOTHER if she does not also have such memories, she says, "Even if Mama had been around, that's not the way it was for us."

"So, how was it?" I persist.

She explains that children were bound to their parents by duty and gratitude. Then she smiles. "Isn't it a pity that all that's changed?"

We have just come back from visiting Big Grandma and are sitting on the porch, drinking iced coffees. "You know, after Mama lost the use of her legs, it became too much for your aunt Tee," Mother begins.

"It would've been too much for anyone," I say.

"Back in the old days, though, we'd have kept her with us till the bitter end." She pauses to sip her coffee, and when she continues, there is an unaccustomed edge to her voice. "Of course, we are free of all that now."

I am remembering our visit to the home. The smell of disinfectant. The freezing air-conditioning. The ancient residents in wheelchairs, lining the sunlit corridor. Today my grandmother thought she was on a ship, headed for somewhere she didn't know. "Where are we going?" she kept asking. "Why are you taking me there?"

My mother gazes out across the lawn and absently stirs the ice cubes in her glass. Finally, she turns to me. "When we are free," she asks, "what holds us then?"

>>>>>><<<<<<

WHILE I AM HOME, my mother cooks. On most mornings, when I come out into the kitchen, she greets me with the question, "What would you like for dinner tonight?" By the time I sit down to my first cup of coffee, she has already hung the laundry, swept and mopped the floors, and is taking a break, clipping recipes from the previous night's paper.

On other days, I wake to the smell of baking. A few mornings before Easter, a wonderful yeasty fragrance fills the whole house, and when I emerge from my bedroom, there are pans of sweet rolls cooling on every available dining surface in the living and dining rooms. Mother reminds me that they are having a bake sale for her General Electric cooking class, and while she was at it, she's decided to make extras to give away. None of it "penance food."

She believes that everything to do with eating should be a pleasure, and she takes as much care in selecting the food she will cook as in its actual preparation. When I am visiting, she rousts me out of bed on Wednesday mornings way before six, so we can get down to the open market when the produce vendors are setting up. Afterward, I drive her to Chinatown , where she is acquainted with the specialties of every shop. She sniffs and pokes, quizzes the vendors about prices, and periodically offers me bits of cryptic advice, like, "Buy fish whole," or "The sound of a pineapple tells you if it's sweet."

AFTER MY RETURN TO MICHIGAN, Mother and I continue to keep in frequent touch. On one occasion, she reports that Big Grandma has now decided that she is visiting at her uncle's estate back in Japan. "She seems happier," Mother says. "But the last time I saw her, she complained of what a long stay it's been. Then she looked around at her roommate and the other residents out in the hall and whispered, "What are all these people doing here?"

During another call, my mother announces that she and Dad will be coming out to see us the following spring. It will be their first visit since we have moved to the Midwest.

She says, "I told your father that I'll be needing a whole new wardrobe for the trip."

"What you've got is probably fine," I say.

"It's not that." She hesitates. "Nothing fits."

My heart sinks a little. "What do you mean?"

She explains that she's been losing weight, then hastens to assure me, "I've been to the doctor and he's not concerned the slightest bit."

EVERY WEEK SHE CONTINUES to lose another pound or two, but her monthly checkups turn up nothing unusual. She develops a bit of a backache, but both she and her doctor agree that it is just an old muscle strain flaring up.

In late March, when my father and she arrive for their scheduled visit, we are at the airport to meet them. At a distance, we can see them in the crowd, walking from the gate toward us. When I get a clear view, I am startled by the change in her. She is thin, very thin, and her clothes hang loosely on her small frame. Hal and I exchange looks and he squeezes my shoulder reassuringly. Then they spot us, too, and everyone is all smiles, exchanging hugs.

I take to watching her when she's not looking. Her color's good and, even with the weight loss, she does not *look* ill. But she seems to tire easily and her hands tremble, ever so slightly, when she unbuttons her jacket or picks up a pen to write. That night at dinner, the rest of us are passing the wine and helping ourselves to seconds when I notice that she hardly eats—just tiny bitefuls. "Come on, Mother, you've got to do better than that," I say.

She waves me off, but Dad joins in. "Can't keep your strength up if you don't eat."

Even Hal gets into the act and passes the chicken, which she ignores. She takes a tiny biteful of mashed potatoes from her plate.

Hal clears his throat. "So, how's the weather been in Honolulu?" Dad turns to answer him, but I continue watching Mother.

Finally she protests, "You've been staring at me all day. Now cut it out."

SHE IS IN SUCH GOOD SPIRITS that it seems impossible anything can be wrong. She loves our little house. The crocuses blooming in the yard. The unpredictable spring weather. She loves that it can be seventy degrees and sunny one day, and snowing the next. When it starts to snow, she grabs her coat and boots so she can be outside in it. She crunches wet snow into little balls and throws them when my father and I step out the door. I take pictures of the two of them—in the snow on the front walk, in the snow on the side of the house, and in the snow in the backyard. Mother takes naps in the afternoon, but she is always up by dinner. She sits on a stool in the kitchen and watches while I cook. I teach her my recipes for tabouli and refried beans. When we go to the market, she piles the cart with asparagus, just coming into season, and that night we eat it cooked six different ways for our dinner.

She fills me in on the family news. Big Grandma is well, but lives almost entirely in her own world. Tee is baking more mango bread than ever. Esther has recently installed a five-thousand-dollar burglar alarm system, which, she claims, interferes with her telephone. "So whenever you call her, you get a busy signal," Mother explains. "And Esther says, 'If anyone has anything to say to me, they can just come here and tell me in person.'"

One afternoon, Hal drives us all to Lake Michigan. It is a forty-minute ride, and on the way over, my mother begins to sing. I remember summer evenings back in the Islands, when it was too hot to stay inside, and she and I went for drives along the sea. Then in the middle of telling me about some dance she'd been to when she was young, she'd start to sing, and I'd join in. We'd both sing, riding the night roads, all the way home.

A FEW WEEKS AFTER my parents return to Honolulu, Mother takes to her bed. Her back is worse and she complains of "hunger pains" that don't go away even after she has eaten.

"Does she get out at all?" I ask my father.

"Only to the doctor," he says. "I'm doing all the housework now."

"Who does the cooking?"

There is a silence at the other end. "I do," he finally answers. "But I guess you could say she supervises."

I ask him to put her on the line, and she says, "You're always making such a fuss. There's nothing to be alarmed about."

"Have you thought of getting a second opinion?" I ask.

"A second, third, and fourth...." She laughs. "No one's pushing the panic button."

In the weeks that follow, she continues going from doctor to doctor. They turn up nothing. They do X rays, barium swallows, and CAT scans. One performs an endoscopy and diagnoses gastritis. Another prescribes swimming therapy for her back condition. As long as no one mentions cancer, we are cheered by every diagnosis, but the weight continues slipping off.

I tell my father, "You have to feed her. We *have* to fatten her up."

And he replies, "She's lost her joy in food."

I begin making plans to fly out there when he calls to say that she has a fever and can't keep anything down.

She picks up the phone before he finishes talking. "Oh, Aya," she says. Her voice comes out in little gasps.

I try not to betray the panic I am feeling. "Just hold on; I'll be there soon. We'll get you better."

Sylvia A. Watanabe »»»×««« 167

"I don't know what's wrong," she says.

These are the last words she speaks to me. That afternoon, my father drives her to the emergency room, and she is rushed into surgery. The doctor finds an abscess covering two-thirds of her liver. He inserts a drainage tube, then closes her up. "I've never seen anything like it," he says.

I FLY BACK THE NEXT DAY. One of my cousins meets me at the airport, and we drive straight to the intensive care unit. My mother is in the same hospital where she had surgery two years before. When we arrive at the waiting room, my father and Aunt Tee are there. I put my arms around my father, who keeps saying, "We've been through this, I just know she's going to get better."

The rules of intensive care allow us to visit my mother in pairs for ten minutes, three times an hour, at twenty-minute intervals. She lies unconscious, with tubes running in and out of her body and a respirator to help her breathe. During one of the breaks between visits, I phone Hal in Michigan, and he says that he'll be with me soon.

Over the next few days, there is no change. Aunt Tee drops by again. The Birthday Girls come. The ladies from the General Electric cooking class bring food for our vigil. One afternoon I am alone with Mother when Aunt Esther enters the room. I look around for Aunt Tee, but Esther has come alone.

"I rode the bus," she says, positioning herself on the other side of the bed.

After we exchange a bit more small talk, I turn back to my mother and pick up where I left off. "Remember the time," I say to her, listing things we've seen and done.

A few minutes go by this way, when Aunt Esther suddenly speaks up; she has been remembering, too. She leans close to Mother's pillow and murmurs, "Remember when we were kids, and you got a new pair of shoes, and I didn't get any? Remember the lady at the corner store who gave you free ice cream that you never shared? Remember how you wanted to tag along wherever I went and how Mama beat me for not taking you?"

THE NEXT MORNING on my way to the ICU, I drop by the senior care wing to see my grandmother. The other residents are at their usual posts along the corridor, but she is parked in the lounge, in front of the TV set, which is playing a rerun of "Lassie."

"Hello, Grandma," I say, kneeling beside her.

She looks up from the image on the screen and peers at me. As I gaze back, it is as if I am looking at her through a one-way mirror. When she speaks, she uses the politest form of Japanese. "And who would you be?"

I begin to explain, then realize, with a kind of grief, that there is no explanation; she will never know anyone again.

I undo the string on the box of sweet bean cakes I have brought, then pass them to her, saying, "I remembered how you like these." Her face creases into a smile as she takes one out and bites into it. Then she offers one to me, and we sit for a while, eating quietly together. "This is a rare thing," she says, "Yes, this is a rare thing."

MORE DAYS PASS. Hal arrives. The doctors move Mother out of intensive care. It's not looking good, they say. The antibiotics aren't working, and the infection is in her blood.

In the new room, we can be with her all the time. We stand by the bed, massaging her icy hands and feet. Dad quits talking about miracle recoveries. One afternoon, while Hal is getting a cup of coffee and I am half-dozing in a chair across the room, I can hear my father talking to her. "It's okay, Betty," he is saying. "You can let go now. You can let go."

None of our friends or relatives come by anymore. There is a sign on the door that says, VISITORS LIMITED TO IMMEDIATE FAMILY. I sense that it is difficult for my father to be there; the air-conditioning, the hours of sitting on a hard chair are bad for his arthritis, so I tell him that it's all right if he leaves early because we'll call if anything happens.

When the nurses come to change the bedding, they instruct Hal and me to wear rubber gloves whenever we touch my mother. This is to safeguard against infection from the fluids leaking out of her. Periodically, someone stops by to vacuum her mouth and throat with a suction device on the side of the bed. The necessity for doing this becomes more and more frequent, and finally, one of the nurses shows me how to do it. There is the smell of blood, perhaps of earth, around my mother's bed.

With just my husband there in the room with us, I sing to her. She lies in the same position she's been in, with her head turned to one side, and one leg slightly bent, as if she's dancing. I sing, "Sunset glow the day is over, let us all go home...." I close my eyes, and imagine myself large—large enough to hold all of her, her dying, within me.

HAL AND I HAVE RENTED a room in the medical center where we can take quick naps during the day or grab a few hours of sleep at night. The room is in the same wing as the senior care facility, a floor below my grandmother's. At one or two in the morning, after a day of sitting with my mother, he and I squeeze into the narrow, twin-size bed, and still in our street clothes, almost immediately fall asleep. We have slept less than an hour when we are wakened by a banging on the door. We stumble to our feet, and I feel as if I've plunged into a pool of icy water. I am so cold, my teeth are chattering, and it is difficult to catch my breath. Hal steadies me, then opens the door. There are two nurses on the other side. They tell us, in a businesslike way, to go to my mother's room. As we follow them down the corridor, I think of Big Grandma somewhere upstairs, wakeful, among strangers.

David Wojahn

DAVID WOJAHN is the author of five collections of poetry, *Icehouse Lights* (1982), which was a selection in the Yale Series of Younger Poets and a winner of the William Carlos Williams Book Award, as well as *Glassworks* (1987), *Mystery Train* (1990), *Late Empire* (1994), and *The Falling Hour* (1997)—all published by the University of Pittsburgh Press. He is also the author of *Strange Good Fortune*, a collection of essays on contemporary poetry, which will be published by the University of Arkansas Press in 2001. He is Lilly Professor of Poetry and Director of the Program in Creative Writing at Indiana University, and also a member of the faculty in the MFA in Writing Program at Vermont College.

A Cavalier and Doomed Lot:
James L. White, A Memoir

>>>>>>>>>>>>>>>>>>>>>X<<<<<<<<<<<<<<<<<<<<

The poet James L. White has now been dead for sixteen years, killed in his sleep—by a heart attack—in Minneapolis in the summer of 1981. He was the author of four collections of poetry, and his work has suffered the fate one might expect of a good but finally minor poet: a few people still read him, and certain poets of my own generation can be said to have been influenced by him, though none of his books remain in print. *Good but minor:* it is a description I employ with caution, for I do not mean it to be pejorative. Weldon Kees is good but minor, and several of his poems I know by heart. Good but minor is a category that includes many poets whose work I love: Thomas Traherne, John Clare, Ivor Guemey, Lorrine Neidecker, and John Logan come to mind. But my purpose here is not to evaluate the poetry of James L. White, though I plan to discuss certain of his poems in detail. Nor is it to draw some hairsplitting distinction between major and minor (is Kees a minor-major poet or a major-minor poet?), especially when I fear that my own poetic career may not even qualify me for a place in one of the farm-clubs of Parnassus.

What I instead intend to discuss is something more perplexing and intricate, for James L. White was my poetic mentor, and it is to him I owe many of my notions about the practice and teaching of poetry. In talking about Jim, I want also to discuss the issue of mentoring, a subject that has recently been of some interest to me, if only because the dynamics of mentoring are curious ones, subject to few strict rules. Mentoring is also a tale likely to produce an unhappy ending: it is a story which begins in nurture but which tends to end in rejection or loss. Yet good stories rarely possess happy endings. If the relationship of a mentor to his/her disciple can be likened to that of a parent to a child, it should come as no surprise that the end of mentoring is that we become our mentors, in the same way that it is my late father's face that stares at me from the mirror each morning. Yet I am not my father. When I set a poem down in my notebook or on the screen of my laptop, I sometimes feel that it is the presence of James L. White that helps guide my pen or fingertips. Yet I am not Jim White, although I now am nearly as old as Jim White at the time of his own death. When, then, does mentoring end? And when it ends, what then are we left with? Jim White, like so many of those who have meant the most to me, now dwells among the shades, and it is said that the shades seek for themselves only the balm of forgetfulness; they are indifferent to our eulogies, indifferent to our problems. That I conjure him for selfish reasons should come as no surprise.

I first met Jim White twenty-two years ago, on a snowy November night in Minnesota. Two friends and I were coordinating a series of poetry readings by local writers at a neighborhood community center, which had been funded, after a couple of years of existence, by the State Arts Board with a princely grant of $500; with this, donations, and money from our own pockets, we could pay our readers a $50 honorarium. James L. White, whose work I had known from the local poetry scene and his two small-press books, had agreed to read on the night in question, but it did not seem likely that the reading, which he was to give with another local poet, James Moore, was going to take place. Nearly a foot of snow had fallen, and so the first time I ever spoke with Jim was during my phone call to suggest we cancel the reading. Jim, however, would have none of it, and so the reading took place that night with six or seven people in attendance, the wind and snow battering the windows behind the podium, though the scene was far from dramatic. There's always something embarrassing about a poetry reading before an audience as tiny as the one that had gathered that night; readers tend to respond to the intimacy of such situations by retreating into shyness and quietude. Not so with Jim White, who read a group of his newer poems in a highly intense and mellifluous fashion; it wasn't the booming sort of declamatory reading I'd come to expect from Midwestern writers of that era such as the then-ubiquitous Robert Bly. The performance was far more controlled and far less rhetorical and stagy than that. More importantly, though, the poems were powerful and emotionally gripping, like nothing I had heard before from a local poet, where the prevailing style aimed for a bland and mildly surrealist miniature: little epiphanies in cornfields were the norm.

How different these poems were from the first poem that Jim read that night, and which was later included in his posthumous collection, *The Salt Ecstacies*:

Summer News

Transients loiter in downtown parks with
the stillness of foxes.
One smiles as if I knew him near a fountain
in his center of light,
wearing a faded shirt like summer news.

His body invites conversation.
They threaten tornadoes through the city as
hunters and prey agree on common shelter.

The storm enters our skin gathering
as we begin the familiar gestures.

In his room I speak of death, its promise of ending.
He undresses me, telling me how tired I am,
that friends have brought me their truths all day.
He seems as beautiful as I wish my life was
in the boiling light of our slight sweating.

Now the old blues
before the bad gin and storm.
We vow total selfishness
and we begin to touch
and we begin to rain...[1]

What's immediately striking about this poem, both twenty years ago and as I read it today, is the honesty and directness of its content. No hermeticism and vaguely Jungian musings here. The poem is direct in its narrative and unabashedly "out"—and to write openly of gay sexuality in those days, even in a supposed bastion of liberality such as Minnesota, was to violate a number of aesthetic taboos. Yet the valor of the poem derives from other factors as well. Its diction achieves a delicate equipoise between simplicity and adamant lyrical flourish: The plaintive and almost embarrassingly bald "he seems as beautiful as I wish my life was" is followed by the exquisitely modulated consonance of "in the boiling light of our slight sweating." And this, in turn, is followed by the clipped and weary "Now the old blues / before the bad gin and storm..."—huge shifts in diction abound in the poem, but their effect is seamless. Furthermore, the poem's narrative evolves with a strict and evocative delicacy: There's the erotic charge of the initial encounter in the park, followed by the tender (yet furtive and almost desperate) scene of the two men in the apartment. The poem's imagery—the repeated references to water and storm as both erotic life force and a kind of terrifying deluge—is insistent but unobtrusive. The poem's language and motifs combine to create what is often the most memorable aspect of Jim's best poems, a speaking voice astonishingly vulnerable, strikingly idiosyncratic, and for the most part shorn of self-pity. The models for this style seem to me two poets also admired for this sort of speaking voice, Cavafy and James Wright. It's not merely the homoerotic subject matter of the poem which recalls Cavafy, but also a language that rapidly shifts between an incantatory formality and an idiomatic flatness. The echoes of Wright can be heard in the poem's imagery and in a kind of deadpan exposition. (Compare the opening of "Summer News" to certain middle-period Wright poems such as "The Poor Washed Up by Chicago Winter" or "Inscription for the Tank.") One's choice of models of course says a lot about a writer, and Cavafy and Wright are difficult masters, precisely because of the deceptive simplicity of their manners.

The other poems that Jim read that night shared these qualities, and some of them later appeared (in different form, for Jim was a pains-taking reviser) in *The Salt Ecstacies*. The most notable of them was a long fuguelike poem, reminiscent of Lorca's bullfighter elegy, entitled "The Clay Dancer." The poem mixes the psalmic and liturgical surrealism of Lorca's poem with a series of autobiographical vignettes centered on sexual awakening and coming out. The method is audacious, and more so even than in "Summer News," the poem successfully mixes a galvanic and fluent music with a plainspoken vulnerability. Yet the most startling aspect of the poem is that we are asked to read it as Jim's self-elegy: The protagonist seems, in a bizarre mixture of *Sunset Boulevard* and any number of Hardy poems, to be addressing us and himself from the grave. Its self-elegizing ranges from tenderness to the most brutal sort of

David Wojahn »»»»««« 177

chastisement. It is a frightening and morbidly prophetic piece of work, snarling in its self-interrogation but scored with the stately solemnities of requiem. Perhaps every good poet must eventually write a version of "Ode to a Nightingale," and "The Clay Dancer" was Jim's. It was the last thing Jim read that night, and our little group, huddled around the podium as snow beat against the windowpanes, received the close of the poem with a kind of entranced collective silence. Minutes seemed to pass before the applause began.

My friendship with Jim White began on that evening. I was twenty-three, and Jim was just shy of forty. My life had thus far been an uneventful and sheltered product of Midwestern suburbia, and though Jim and I shared Midwestern backgrounds—he'd grown up in Indianapolis—his life had been anything but uneventful. He'd in fact lived several lives. Jim's first passion was the dance, and shortly after his sixteenth birthday he won a scholarship to study in New York in the American Ballet Theater. He then danced professionally with several troupes, both here and in Europe, served briefly in the navy, received English degrees from Indiana University and Colorado State, and then, toward the end of the 1960s, headed for the Southwest, where he lived for several years among the Navajo and Hopi, first as a teacher, and later as the artistic director of a Native American theater group based in New Mexico.

By the time I met him, he had been in Minnesota for several years, teaching in the Writers-in-the-Schools program, mostly in reservation schools. It was the sort of itinerant existence, traveling from school to school around the state for little money, to which Jim had by this point in his life grown accustomed. I doubt that he regarded this chronicle of wanderings and rootlessness as a romantic one, however. He was, no doubt, a good dancer, but not talented enough to turn it into a lifelong career. And his involvement with Native Americans, long-standing as it was, could never change his status as an outsider among those cultures. Even as a poet, he dwelled outside the pale, never willing to sell himself for the purpose of landing an easy academic position, and never fitting very comfortably into a provincial literary community whose values and ambitions were quite different from his own. Finally, as a gay writer from a generation born too early to reap the benefits of the post-Stonewall era, he felt acutely the cost of coming out. The epigraph to *The Salt Ecstacies* is an ominous quotation from Leviticus: "Whosoever liveth with these scars / shall dwell outside the tribe." For the vulnerable and shy Jim White, obsessed as he clearly was with the desire for a community—whether of artists, tribal peoples, or fellow gays—there was no clan in which to truly dwell, and his deeply contingent honorary memberships in the communities he sought only served to remind him of his difference. Jim thought his life of wandering had also been one of the reasons for his frail health. He believed that the physical punishments of the dancer's life had helped to cause the angina that would prove fatal to him—though Jim's history of sporadic substance abuse might also have been a factor.

My friendship with Jim began at a point of important transition in his life. He had entered middle age with a vague but emphatic sense that he did not have long to live. His existence had been full but rootless, and he was coming to suspect, after a series of unhappy love affairs, that it was also a life in which solitude would be his destiny. I think he was also troubled by the suspicion that in his various lives he had displayed talent in many disciplines but had achieved mastery of none. He had now been publishing his poems for the better part of a decade, but the voice of his first two collections—they appeared in 1972 and '74—is neither his own nor very interesting, and Jim must have known this. Although some of the poems display a precise and deftly lyric engagement with the landscape of the Southwest and with Native American cultures, their speaker is self-effaced to the point of concealment, and the poems, finally, never begin to get off the ground.

Jim White, at forty, was not undergoing a midlife crisis, but was instead experiencing the throes of something far more intense: I suppose the best term for it is a crisis of the soul, a *noche oscura*. He confronted this condition in some of the era's expected ways, of course: He'd stopped his drinking and drug use, and had engaged in an intense study of Zen Buddhism; he'd started visiting a therapist. But the greatest change took place in Jim's poetry. Suddenly the poems mattered. Like "Summer News," Jim's new poems were starkly self-confrontational, sure in their music, and stamped with an urgency that his work had never before possessed. The poems were keeping Jim alive: I make this statement with full awareness of its hyperbolic implications, yet in Jim's case no other characterization will suffice. I have known a handful of other writers who were sustained by poetry in this way, for whom the craft went beyond self-expression or self-therapy and became instead a kind of life-support system. They are figures to whom we must respond with a mixture of awe and sorrow, for I doubt if theirs is a condition we would wish upon those we love. But such was to be Jim White's fate.

This is not to say I knew any of this as I began, in the months after I met Jim, to foist my poems upon him. Like most young poets, I craved attention, and like most young poets I had no idea whether my work was good. This was a blissful ignorance, surely, because if I had suspected just how ghastly my work really was I probably would have given up on it. But I was wholly intoxicated by poetry, reading every collection of contemporary verse I could find, and trying my hand at every conceivable period style: I was Olson on one day, Merwin on the next, and never patient enough to let my poems go beyond my borrowed styles' surface mannerisms. I had taken some writing classes at the University of Minnesota with the expatriate British poet Michael Dennis Browne, who was a charismatic and generous teacher. But I felt more an autodidact than a student, and possessed an autodidact's mixture of arrogance and confusion. I had the good fortune to have taken a night watchman's job, working four nights a week alone in a large medical building. It gave me plenty of time to read and write, and so the Lowery Medical Arts building became my classroom, where I'd churn out poems and, perhaps even more importantly, weekly book reviews for the university student paper, *The Minnesota Daily*. Fiction, biography, criticism, and especially poetry—the editors let me write about anything I chose, and in the pages of the *Daily* I worked out my opinions about many writers who would grow essential for me: Ashbery, Wright, Cavafy, Ritsos, Pavese, as well as younger writers such as Norman Dubie and Heather McHugh. I doubt if these pieces were very perceptive, but I quickly mastered the reviewer's art of making myself look smart, and I reveled in my newfound sense of power. I was an opinion-maker! Writers of the books I reviewed even wrote notes of thanks and (sometimes) condemnation to me. "Dear David Wojahn," wrote Heather McHugh on the occasion of my review of her first book, "if all the pans are as bright as yours, I will be well-fried." My apprenticeship to this point was an odd one: I was laboring in solitude, as I thought a poet should. But my ambitions were decidedly po-biz.

Over the next two years, until I left Minnesota for graduate school, Jim White became my tutor, though I doubt if we would have described our relationship in such formal terms. Every few weeks I'd meet with him, in coffee shops or in his apartment, and show him my poems. His place was small and sparely furnished, just a pair of living room chairs, a kitchen table, and on the floor his antique Navajo rug, the only one of his possessions that he claimed to be proud of. I remember little of our conversations, save that he listened with care as I read him my work and that he annotated the poems carefully, in a spidery cursive. From time to time he'd offer a few suggestions for revising the poems, yet Jim was not the sort of teacher who was given to pronouncements. I remember nothing specific about his comments, and I'm sure that even the most pointed of suggestions wouldn't have helped to salvage my wretched scribblings. What counted for more, although I only dimly perceived it then, was Jim's gracious *attentiveness* to the poems. He read them as if they were worthy of respectful attention. I have no idea why Jim chose to honor my poems in this way. Perhaps his newfound seriousness about his own work had given him a similar stance toward the work of others, even a tyro such as myself. Perhaps he recognized some talent in me, or at least some requisite ambition that could be different from mere careerism. Perhaps, too, it was gratifying for him to know that a young poet respected his work and opinions in the way that I so clearly did. At any rate, I had found a mentor. A mentor, not a teacher. Not someone paid to offer advice, but someone who, in the awkward and mysteriously reciprocal fashion in which mentoring seems to be enacted, helped to bring me to a clearer awareness of what it meant to write poems. Jim gave me instruction and advice, of course, but also, and perhaps more importantly, he showed me kindness, a quality which does not exist these days in much abundance. Yet it is kindness such as Jim displayed, this scrupulous philanthropy of expertise, which counted the most in our relationship, more so, I think, than the actual usefulness of his advice.

It goes without saying that mentors needn't give the best advice in order to be of crucial value. Literary history provides countless cases of well-intentioned mentors who offer useless or even damaging counsel to their charges: Maudlin Leigh Hunts, trigger-happy Verlaines, and boneheaded Thomas Higginsons abound. And, as the example of Verlaine so pathetically illustrates, mentors can often change into lovers, Svengalis, or ego-trippers, to the detriment of both mentor and disciple. Surely there are some literary mentorings that can survive such complications. The tryst between Louise Bogan and her much younger admirer Theodore Roethke is bracingly described by Bogan's biographer Elizabeth Frank as a liaison that "evolved, through distance, tact, and a recognition of the circumstances of each other's lives, into one of those bonds which closely resembles a love affair, namely, an intense mutual attachment between student and teacher."[2] This sounds like a much more fruitful pattern than the more typical scenario of middle-age professors hitting on their students! Perhaps just as drably typical is the tendency of mentors to break with disciples when the disciples come into their own as artists, and in doing so appear to reject their mentors' counsel and example. Alan Tate, for whom autobiographical poems were anathema, was profoundly distressed by the confessional verse of his one-time student Robert Lowell: "But Cal," wrote Tate to Lowell upon the publication of *Life Studies*, "it's not *poetry*." In David Kalstone's *Becoming a Poet*, his brilliant analysis of Elizabeth Bishop's literary friendships with Marianne Moore and Lowell, we see the erosion of mentoring in sadly vivid detail. Moore's championing of Bishop's work for the most part ended after Bishop refused to adopt the revisions that Moore had suggested for Bishop's "Roosters," and a good thing it was that Bishop would not be swayed. Moore offered Bishop a bizarrely revised version of the poem, one that mangled the delicacy of its triple rhyme stanzas, bowdlerized vocabulary that Moore deemed indelicate—"water closet" seems to have offended Moore, though, ironically, she naively suggested that Bishop might change her title to "The Cock." She sought to turn a subtle psychological allegory of sexual outsiderhood and survival into a merely descriptive word machine: a modernist poem such as one of Moore's, in other words. After the "Roosters" fiasco, nothing was ever the same between the two. "The rift," writes Kalstone, "was more startling than its comic origins suggest. Recalling the farrago years later, Bishop said she never again sent Moore any of her poems for suggestions or approval."[3]

So artistic mentors may give bad advice, may in fact give dangerous advice. And how, furthermore, does a disciple distinguish between the mentor's message and the example of the mentor's own life? Kappus was fortunate to have known Rilke only through his *Letters to a Young Poet*, and thus was not presented with the insufferable high-class gigolo who was in fact the letters' author. Or is it instead *regrettable* that Kappus did not encounter Rilke in his Euro-trash aspect, Rilke as sycophant and dead-beat dad? Perhaps it is better to see the chinks in our mentors' armor, and to see them early. Mentoring is a complicated business because it is conducted always in a state of unease. The disciple wants to be changed by the mentor, changed utterly. Yet the self is more likely to resist such change than to welcome it. Michael Heller, in a canny memoir about his mentor George Oppen, puts it this way: "The uneasiness of poetic interrelation, of 'influence' (as Harold Bloom might inflect the word) lies buried in the factorials of poetic learning. Every transmission from 'mentor' to student abrades the self's inertial desires to maintain the fiction of its own 'gracefulness,' its own completeness."[4] I imagine that I first sought Jim White's advice because I wanted someone to listen to me, to praise me, to coddle my bumbling and misshapen poetic aspirations. But what I was given by Jim was instead an education in the emotional and spiritual costliness of poetic endeavor. Success, happiness, and security all proved elusive for Jim. And through Jim I came to see how likely such a fate can be for a serious poet in our era. Not the inevitable fate, surely, but a fate shared by others like Jim who I have since known, and known well. Yet it need not be considered a cruel and unjust fate. I am reminded of the painter Donald Evans, who wrote that his life was about "the *why* of art, and the *I give up* of finding love or happiness." Jim White, more than anyone else I have known, showed me the *why* of art.

I first dimly perceived this as Jim's essential message one afternoon when I was visiting him in his apartment. He read me a draft of the poem destined to open *The Salt Ecstacies*. Like several of Jim's best poems, it is an ars poetica of an urgently expressive sort:

An Ordinary Composure

I question what poetry will tremble the wall into hearing or tilt the stone angel's slight wings at words of the past like a memory caught in elms. We see nothing ahead. My people and I lean against great medical buildings with news of our predicted death, and give up mostly between one and three in the morning, never finding space large enough for a true departure, so our eyes gaze earthward, wanting to say something simple as *the meal's too small: I want more.* Then we empty from a room on intensive care into the sea, releasing our being to the slap of waves.

Poems break down here at the thought of arms never coupling into full moons by holding those we love again, and so we resort to the romantic: a white horse, set quivering like a slab of marble into dancing flesh.

Why remember being around a picnic table over at Brookside Park? We played softball that afternoon. My mother wore her sweater in the summer because of the diabetes. Night blackened the lake like a caught breath. We packed things up. I think I was going to school that fall or a job somewhere. Michael'd go to Korea. Before we left I hit the torn softball into the lake and Michael said, "You can't do that for shit James Lee."

Going back, I realized the picnic was for us. It started raining in a totally different way, knowing we'd grow up right on into wars and trains and deaths and loving people and leaving them and being left and being alone.

That's the way of my life, the ordinary composure of loving, loneliness, and death, and too these prayers at the waves, the white horse shimmering, bringing it toward us out of coldest marble.[5]

As with "Summer News," what we first notice about the poem is its mixing of dictions. The high rhetoric of the opening clause is followed by the quirky surrealism of the sentence's conclusion, which is in turn followed by the gruff flatness of "we see nothing ahead." Then comes the eerie meditation on mortality that concludes the opening paragraph. (By this time Jim's doctors had diagnosed his heart condition as inoperable, and likely to be fatal.) The contrast drawn between the certainty of mortality and blandishments of art is amplified in paragraph two, but suddenly the poem departs from these motifs entirely. The memory of the picnic is described reportorially, almost casually. This in turn prepares us for the even flatter vocabulary of paragraph four, yet in the context of the poem's quirky musicality the disarmingly plain language of a passage such as "we'd grow right on up into wars and trains and death and loving people and leaving them" has the effect of revelation. When the poem returns in its final sentence to its speculations on the art of poetry, the dichotomy between art and life that the poem has struggled with is now obliterated—not resolved, exactly, but transformed into a haunted stasis. I needn't add that such a poem is difficult to bring off; Jim struggled through many drafts to get the tone right, to find the proper mixture of lyric and demotic. A version of the poem published in a quarterly is considerably different from the one which eventually appeared in *Salt Ecstacies*.

I remember my feelings of astonishment when Jim read me this poem. I was flattered that Jim had decided to ask me for his advice with his work, and it signaled, I think, a turning point in our relationship. From that day on, it seemed that Jim regarded me as his peer and confidante as much as his student, and in perceiving my new role I felt honored, admitted to the writerly company at last. This is not to say our new relationship was uncomplicated. Jim's vulnerability and hypersensitive devotion to the art could sometimes turn to mere peevishness and even to a kind of paranoia. The burden of his life of wanderings and his deep loneliness was now wearing heavily upon him. His devotion to his writing seemed not to translate into any sort of public recognition: He continued to feel that he labored in obscurity within a backwater literary community that could not appreciate his new work. Jim also believed that many of his straight friends had cooled to him when he chose to come out. He, in turn, severed his ties with them. As one of the poems of *The Salt Ecstacies* laments, "I have left so many this year / who felt too comfortable with my old design."

Like so many gay men of his generation, he chose to hide his gayness from his family. He was deeply devoted to his sister and his aging mother, who knew that Jim was a poet, but Jim never told them about the publication of *The Del Rio Hotel*, his third book, and the first of his collections to overtly treat gay themes. About *The Salt Ecstacies*, the collection that meant so much to him, they seemed also to have known nothing, at least while Jim was alive. Although he ostensibly remained as gentle-tempered and gracious as he had ever been, Jim became increasingly isolated and dejected in his "new design." Meanwhile, Jim's poems grew even more urgent and risky. Darkly retrospective, and increasingly imbued with Jim's awareness of his mortality, the poems seem at once both personal and prophetic. For whatever reasons, Jim felt that I could serve as a first reader and audience for many of these poems; and sometimes it seemed as though Jim feared that his audience would never grow beyond that of myself and a handful of his other friends. Jim's last years became an ever-increasing struggle against the fear that he would die with his mission as a poet incomplete, and with his work unread. Increasingly, Jim's small inner circle of friends was composed of those who it seemed to him comprehended his absolute devotion to this struggle, and to accept its mixture of integrity, asceticism, and desperation. To be Jim's friend at this point was often a bit of a challenge. As one of Jim's few straight male friends, I was asked to lend a disinterested ear to Jim's tales of his infatuations, and troubled love affairs, which tended to end badly. Of course I was too young and inept to offer any useful counsel. Several times Jim felt he was on the verge of forming a lasting partnership with one of his lovers, but in every case these liaisons faltered. By the end of his life, Jim's sexual encounters were limited to anonymous couplings in a Hennipen Avenue bathhouse— this was several years before the emergence of AIDS—a place where I'd often drop him off, for Jim never learned to drive, after our dinners or meetings to discuss our poems. As Jim resigned himself to the *I give up* of finding love, however, his obsession with the *why* of art grew more pervasive, in both good ways and bad. On the one hand, his poems grew more stark, Cavafian, and heartbreaking. "Making Love to Myself," both rhapsodic in its eroticism and a work of the deepest resignation, is Jim's version of Cavafy poems such as "Days of 1908" and "The Bandaged Shoulder":

Making Love to Myself

When I do it I remember how it was with us.
Then my hands remember too,
and you're with me again, just the way it was.

After work you'd come in and turn the TV off and sit on the edge
of the bed,

filling the room with gasoline smell from your overalls,
trying not to wake me which you always did.
I'd breathe out long and say,
'Hi Jess, you tired, baby?'
You'd say not so bad and rub my belly,
not after me, really, just being sweet,
and I always thought I'd die a little
because you smelt like burnt leaves or woodsmoke.

We were poor as Job's turkey but we lived well—
the food, a few good movies, good dope, lots of talk,
lots of you and me trying on each other's skin.

What a sweet gift this is,
done with my memory, my cock and hands.

Sometimes I'd wake up wondering if I should fix
coffee for us before work,
almost thinking you're here again, almost seeing
your work jacket on the chair.

I wonder if you remember what
we promised when you took that job in Laramie?
Our way of staying with each other.
We promised there'd always be times
when the sky was perfectly lucid,
that we could remember each other through that.
You could remember me at my worktable
or in the all-night diners,
though we'd never call or write.

I have to stop here Jess.
I just have to stop.[6]

As with Cavafy's erotic poems, the portraiture here is spare but intensely cast, and the poem's narrative framework—the masturbatory fantasy as the catalyst for the story of the couple's relationship—helps to create the plainspoken but very surprising and affecting turn in the poem's final stanza. In its combination of minimalism and madrigal-like grace notes, it is perhaps the most characteristic of Jim's later poems. But it is also the sort of poem that had no place in the mainstream of American poetry in the late 1970s.

Jim finished *The Salt Ecstacies* around 1978, thanks largely to a writing grant from the Bush Foundation. He had great hopes for the book, but his efforts at finding a publisher for it looked as though they would come to nothing. Jim was obsessed with the hope that the book would be brought out by a major publisher. The small presses that released Jim's previous work could never offer Jim the sort of distribution and readership he craved for *The Salt Ecstacies*. He feared that even if he were to offer the book to one of these presses that the editors would blanche at the newfound sexual frankness of a poet who had previously been identified with a mere picturesque regionalism. He felt equally uneasy with the possibility of sending the book to a house that specialized in gay poetry—there were very few of them in those days, and he felt that to publish with such a press would ghettoize his work. So Jim engaged in a quixotic mission to have the book appear from a trade house, despite a fear that trade publishers would be even more apt to find his work too specialized, too gay. The commercial presses were for the most part uninterested, of course. But in two or three instances it seemed that Jim looked close to being offered a contract. These rejections, coming after Jim had allowed his hopes to soar, were especially painful, and he railed against a pair of editors who he felt had led him on, and against the work of poets these editors had taken on instead of Jim. Such a chronicle of rejection is typical for even the best of contemporary poets, but it went on at the same time as Jim's health continued its precipitous decline. His heart attacks grew more frequent, and on more than one occasion he found himself opening his rejection slips after his mail had been brought to him in intensive care. *The Salt Ecstacies* had become Jim's sole legacy.

By this time I had moved away from Minneapolis to attend graduate school in Arizona and because one of my teachers there, the poet Tess Gallagher, had been a judge for the Bush Foundation grant that Jim had received, he enlisted me in the struggle with *Salt*. He'd had another heart attack, and called me one day shortly after he'd been released from the hospital. Would I make a copy of *Salt Ecstacies* and give it to Tess? Perhaps she could use her connections to help Jim find a publisher for the book. So that week I went to Tess's office with the manuscript, explaining something of Jim's situation, and asking if she'd read the collection and write Jim with her appraisal. Having remembered Jim's work from the Bush competition, she eagerly agreed to look at the manuscript, and, over the next few years, became a tireless champion of Jim's work. She not only read the book, but also offered Jim a flurry of editorial advice: not just regarding the arrangement of the poems, but also line-by-line criticism of almost all of the manuscript's efforts. In some cases she suggested fairly radical alterations for the poems, most of which Jim adopted. Although many of her suggestions now seem to me a bit ill-advised—Jim's early versions of certain of the poems strike me as more elegant and musical than those which emerged after Tess's blue-pencilings—the best of her advice was superb, especially in regard to matters of style: Her edits helped Jim's tonal and dictional shifts, one of his greatest strengths, to seem even more abrupt and surprising. Just as importantly, I think, Tess became a supportive correspondent; the two began a regular and affectionate exchange of letters that continued until Jim's death. Thanks to

Tess's encouragement and promises to help him find a publisher for *The Salt Ecstacies*, he went back to his poems with a renewed vigor, dropping a number of less successful pieces from the manuscript and adding a small number of new poems.

One of these new poems Jim read to me when we met during one of my visits home, and was inspired by a conversation Jim had recently had with his cardiologist, a former navy doctor, who had in his youth worked in a military hospital for tertiary syphilitics. Given that so many of Jim's recent poems had alluded to illness, the title of the poem, "Syphilis Prior to Penicillin," came as no surprise. But that the poem, like "An Ordinary Composure," asked to be read as an ars poetica, came as a considerable surprise:

Syphilis Prior to Penicillin

The United States Coast Guard had a
hospital for it in New York until 1952.
My doctor said if you knew syphilis
you knew medicine because it
perfectly imitated other diseases.

That in the last stages when it went rampant,
(beside their minds)
sailors would lose a nose or ear,
the disease mimicking leprosy.
And it was never cured or stabilized
so the sailors carried themselves as
loaded weapons into every port.

The whores could never really tell either
for they were eaten with it too.

Those who knew their condition
often banded together
trying not to infect others with
a "taste for the mud" as the French say.

They were a cavalier and doomed lot,
trying to hold back the dawn
in their foreign hotels,
where the night porters filled rooms
with verbena and gardenias
to hide the cooking smell of sulfur ointments.

At the last there were signs they couldn't hide.
The motor nerves giving way so they walked with
odd flickering steps. That's why Amelia and Rose Montana
would sit the evening through playing mah-jong,
and the old sailors, Paul and James,
rarely asked the whores to dance.[7]

The off-hand but precise descriptions, and the mixture of wry portraiture and grotesquery, are characteristic of Jim's best work. So too is the poem's empathy for those who "dwell outside the tribe." Whether they be syphilitics, queers, poets, or queer-poets, the poem builds its allegory with a rueful tenderness. "I think," said Jim when he'd read me poem, "that you and I must be Paul and James." The cavalier and doomed lot: Although the label undoubtedly seeks to valorize these roles, it is also slyly ironic. As Jim once put it in a conversation about a mutual friend, "P_____ is too *dumb* to be anything but a poet." Cavalier, doomed, and dumb: in *The Salt Ecstacies* the poem is dedicated to me.

Yet for Jim, *doomed* seemed already the sole way to describe his future. His letters and phone conversations with me showed him even closer to despair about his work. His book continued to be rejected, despite Tess's efforts on Jim's part, despite his recent revisions of the collection. More importantly, Jim's heart condition worsened, and he knew the end was near. He'd made out a will, and though he still continued to sit at zazen, he had also started attending services, renewing his childhood connection to the Episcopal Church. His most serious heart attack yet had occurred in early 1981, and while he was in intensive care another attack took place, during which Jim died: In the minute or two before he was brought back, he had an especially intense near-death experience. He saw himself walking down a long corridor, a huge Anglican cathedral on his left, a long candlelit row of Buddhas on his right. I was living on Cape Cod at that point, and my calls to Jim as he languished in ICU were dispiriting. The drugs he was being given made him sound confused and groggy; he seemed already resigned to what one of his poems describes as giving "silently all and everything into dying."

But a day or two later I heard from Jim again. He had just received a call—put through to him in Intensive Care—from Scott Walker, publisher of Graywolf Press. *The Salt Ecstacies* had finally found a publisher, thanks in large part to Tess's lobbying on the book's behalf. I honestly think that this phone call permitted Jim the four more months he had to live; without it, he would have died on the hospital ward. But now he was permitted what he called "a brief remission," and the knowledge that his book could ensure him a posthumous life.

A few weeks later I was back in Minneapolis, and living there until I could find something to do with my own life. I'd gotten by for the past year on a writing fellowship from the Fine Arts Work Center in Provincetown, but now the fellowship was over and my prospects were nil: no book of my own—though I'd been circulating my manuscript— and no possibility of finding the teaching jobs I'd been applying for. I saw Jim often during this period, and his spirits were for once very high; his health had temporarily stabilized, and he was ecstatic about the pending publication of his book. My own spirits, however, were in the cellar. Yet suddenly, within the space of two days, I'd found a teaching job at the University of New Orleans—it would begin the following autumn—and then was informed by Richard Hugo that my book had been his selection for that year's Yale Younger Poets' Prize. One of the best things about my delight at this good news was to see how pleased it made Jim, who had gone over my manuscript with his usual gentle acuity, and he spoke about my luck with a kind of avuncular glee. We now shared some good fortune, some cause for celebration: the cavalier lot more than the doomed. In June of 1981 it turned out that Jim would finally have a chance to meet Tess Gallagher in person. She was spending the summer in Wisconsin, acting in a friend's independent film project, and had arranged to fly to Minneapolis for a weekend.

I did not suspect it at the time, but this was also Jim's weekend of farewells. We drove to the airport to meet Tess's plane, and at Jim's apartment I watched the two of them spend several hours chattering like long-lost friends. Two incidents from that afternoon stand out. First, Jim hastily rinsed out the cups and teapot of the antique Japanese tea set we were drinking from and presented the pot and two of the cups to Tess. "When you drink from this," he told her, "I want you to fill both cups—and to think of me." It was the sort of sudden sentimental gesture—not to mention a liturgical one!—that I had seen Jim make before, but this time it was accompanied by a kind of solemn gravity that took both Tess and me by surprise. The conversation stalled for a minute. But then Jim's doorbell rang—it was a FedEx courier, bearing the proofs of *The Salt Ecstacies*. We sat around Jim's kitchen table for a while and admired them.

Later the three of us, joined by an ex-student of Tess's who would play host to her for the rest of the weekend, had dinner in a Japanese restaurant, and I dropped Jim off at his apartment. I was probably the last person to see him alive. Two days later, Jim's body was discovered by his friend George Roberts, who had a key to the apartment and was worried when Jim did not answer his phone. He'd died in his sleep. On his bedside table were the proofs of *The Salt Ecstacies*, his glasses folded on top of them. One year after Jim's death, *The Salt Ecstacies* appeared, in a simple and elegant edition. I wish that I could say that the book received attention, but of course even the best books of contemporary poetry are for the most part ignored, and posthumous collections tend to suffer from an even greater neglect. Still, the name of James L. White remains alive. There is, in fact, a tiny but fervent cult. Patricia Hampl has published a wonderfully unmournful and ebullient elegy for him. In 1983, while we were browsing in a Vermont bookstore, I convinced my friend Mark Doty to purchase a copy of *The Salt Ecstacies*, and I am sure that Jim would have been pleased to know that he has influenced the work of one of the principal poets of my generation. Mark's 1991 collection, *Bethlehem in Broad Daylight*, contains a masterful elegy for Jim. It is an ambitious sort of threnody, mixing an autobiographical narrative about the speaker's own coming out with an ardent and celebratory meditation on the meaning of desire. The poem ends with an almost prayerful address to Jim: "And so I want you to wake again / in longing, like the rest of us." Jim would surely have been thrilled to know that one of the better known gay literary magazines is called *The James White Review*. But given the tenor of literary politics in our era, and the financial realities of poetry publishing, Jim's cult will, I fear, always remain a small one. At one point several years ago Kate Green, Jim's literary executor, gave me access to all of Jim's manuscripts and notebooks. We had the notion that there might be enough strong unpublished work to warrant the publication of a collected poems. But only a handful of unpublished and uncollected poems exist, and Jim had for the most part rejected the work that appeared before *The Salt*

Ecstacies. Jim wanted *Salt* to be his sole legacy, and so it will continue to be. Perhaps a time will come when Graywolf or some other publisher will see fit to reprint the book.

Jim's mother, Marie White, whom Jim had written about with such tenderness, lies buried beside him, sharing with Jim a rose-colored granite stone in a vile Indianapolis cemetery. "Together Forever," it reads. The place is huge, and abuts an even larger sprawl of suburban shopping centers and strip malls. From the graveside you can look up beyond the fence to a noisy boulevard of fast food joints and tanning parlors. In this it recalls the graves of my parents in a military cemetery in St. Paul, their gravesite only yards from a cyclone fence which scrapes against the runway lights of Twin Cities International Airport. Look in the opposite direction, and you can see the parking lot of Minnesota's premier tourist attraction, "The World's Largest Shopping Mall." In the Midwest, tawdriness is destiny. And in February, in the Washington Park East Cemetery of Indianapolis, the brown disheveled grass and the equally brown Christmas garlands that still pock so many of the graves, endow the landscape with a starker sort of barrenness, with the "plain sense of things" described in the Stevens poem, a place where it is "difficult even to choose the adjective / for this blank cold."

That Jim, after his career of such unceasing wandering should now lie here, in this bleakest parody of home, seems a final brutal irony. But home, for poets, is the cadence of the written word and not a place. I would like to believe that Jim White's monument is not only the small but graceful mausoleum of *The Salt Ecstacies*, but also his voice as it echoes—faintly and distantly perhaps, but always hauntedly—in the work of those poets who have read him well. It is to Jim White, who urged me to become a poet, and to Lynda Hull—whose finest book also appeared a year after her death, and who showed me during the decade of our marriage what it meant to live as a poet—that I owe my identity as a writer. These shades are my truest and only mentors. That I am the one who can write this, the letters unscrolling blue on the computer screen, seems today a blessing, and I am instructed again to form these words with lapidary care, to be mindful that these characters I shape shall always be written to honor these my teachers, my difficult masters—as legacy, as elegy, as homage. For it is of them, my masters and my masters' words, that I am now composed.

(1996)

Notes

1. James L. White, *The Salt Ecstacies* (St. Paul: Graywolf Press, 1981), p. 23.

2. Elizabeth Frank, *Louise Bogan: A Portrait* (New York: Knopf, 1985), p. 325.

3. David Kalstone, *Becoming a Poet* (New York: Farrar, Straus, & Giroux, 1989), p. 88.

4. Michael Heller, "Mentoring," *Ohio Review* 45 (Winter 1990), p.49.

5. White, p. 9.

6. White, p. 20.

7. White, p. 42.

Excavation Photo

After making love she'd found it, asking me to touch the place
    as well:
her left breast, I remember that precisely, & just below the nipple
    I can also still recall,

half-dollar sized, a dusky pink that grew erect so often in
    my mouth & hands,
But the year, the details of the room, all blown apart in memory,
    broken vessels, potshards

gleaming in the excavation photo's sepia, sunlight & long shadows;
    & if only my hand remains,
circling, pushing, probing, *it's a lump I'm sure of it* & if
    I could tell you what would happen

next, which sound from her throat, which sound from mine, the days
    & weeks to follow
& the bitter eschatologies of touch, what profit would
    such knowledge give you?

Would you hear our bedside clock? Cars outside in the rain?—
    & where is she now? Could you tell me
that much? Sand & gravel sifted & the sought thing rises,
    stroked & circled with a tiny

horsehair brush. Bead, shard, incised bone, it does not flare
    in the toothless worker's

David Wojahn »»»««« 199

whorled palm; & my hand keeps moving even now, the fine
    transparent hairs

erect as they waken from gooseflesh-speckled aureole, my circles
    tight, concentric, *Do you*
feel it now? The push & probe & spiral & the sudden
    yes I can feel it too.

Dana Gioia

DANA GIOIA attended Stanford University and did graduate work at Harvard where he studied with Elizabeth Bishop and Robert Fitzgerald. He left Harvard to attend Stanford Business School. For fifteen years he worked in New York for General Foods (eventually becoming a Vice President) while writing nights and weekends. In 1992 he became a full-time writer. Gioia has published three books of poems—*Daily Horoscope* (1986), *The Gods of Winter* (1991), and *Interrogations at Noon* (2001)—as well as an essay collection, *Can Poetry Matter?* (1992). He has edited a dozen anthologies of poetry and fiction. A prolific critic and reviewer, he is also a regular commentator on BBC Radio. He recently completed *Nosferatu*, an opera libretto, for composer Alva Henderson. Dana Gioia lives in northern California.

Studying with Miss Bishop

>>>>>>>>>>>>>>>>>>><<<<<<<<<<<<<<<<

In February, 1975, I began my last semester as a graduate student in English at Harvard University. Picking my courses that final term, I tried for once to pick them carefully, and I came down to a choice between two teachers—Robert Lowell and Elizabeth Bishop. Mr. Lowell's seminar on nineteenth-century poets was very popular. Everyone who fanced himself a poet talked about taking it. As for Elizabeth Bishop's course on modern poetry, I had never heard anyone mention it at all. It seemed to exist only in the course catalogue: "English 285: Studies in Modern Poetry: Miss Elizabeth Bishop, Instructor."

In retrospect, one might imagine that it would have been nearly impossible to get into one of Elizabeth Bishop's classes. But this was not the case. Her course was not one of the many that Harvard students fought to get into and afterward always managed to mention they had taken. The most popular teachers among the young literary elite were Robert Lowell, William Alfred, Robert Fitzgerald, and the newly arrived Alexander Theroux. On the first day of their classes, it was difficult just to squeeze into the room. While Northrop Frye, who was visiting Harvard that year to deliver the Norton Lectures, drew audiences of nearly a thousand for his class on myth and literature, Miss Bishop, I was to learn, rarely attracted more than a dozen unenthusiastic undergraduates. Her manner was at odds with the academic glamour of Harvard, her conversation not designed to impress. She was a politely formal, shy, and undramatic woman. She wanted no worshipful circle of students, and got none. Only her writing course was popular, but all writing courses were in great demand at Harvard, since the university as a matter of policy offered very few. While the Cambridge literary establishment held Miss Bishop in the highest esteem, among the undergraduates she was just another writer on the faculty. They knew she was well known, but wasn't everyone who taught at Harvard?

Miss Bishop's first session was held in a classroom on the second floor of Sever Hall, a grimy building of supposed architectural distinction in the Harvard Yard. The classroom—narrow, poorly whitewashed, with high, cracked ceilings—looked as if it belonged in an abandoned high school in North Dakota. There were exposed radiator pipes with peeling paint. A few battered shelves were lined with broken-spined textbooks of incalculable age. A couple of dozen chairs, no two of them matching, were set randomly around a huge, scratched table, at one end of which—prim, impeccably coiffured, and smoking—sat Miss Elizabeth Bishop.

I recognized her immediately from photographs I had seen in books, but somehow, suddenly coming into a room where she was sitting a few feet away, I was taken by surprise. At that point in my life, I had seen so few real poets in person that I felt a strange shock at being in the same room as someone whose work I knew on the page. It was an odd, almost uncomfortable sensation to have the perfect world of books peer so casually into the disorder of everyday life. I was also surprised by her appearance. She seemed disappointingly normal. I don't know exactly what I had expected—perhaps someone slightly bohemian or noticeably eccentric, a Marianne Moore or a Margaret Rutherford. Instead, I saw a very attractive woman in what I guessed to be her middle fifties (actually, she was sixty-four), dressed in a tasteful, expensive-looking suit, perfectly poised, waiting to begin. By the time the class started, only about a dozen students had arrived. I was surprised at so small a turnout. Moreover, we sat scattered around the room in a way that made the class seem half empty rather than intimate.

Eventually, she began. "I am Elizabeth Bishop," she announced, "and this is Studies in Modern Poetry. The way I usually run this class is by asking the students to choose three or four poets they would like to read and talk about. Does anyone have a suggestion?"

The first question was always an important moment in a Harvard class. It set the tone of the session, like the opening bid on the New York Stock Exchange.

"Can we read John Ashbery? Something like 'Self-Portrait in a Convex Mirror'?" a young man asked from the back of the room.

Now, this was a truly exceptional question. Ashbery was just becoming well known, and every young poet I knew had been reading him. But hardly anyone was able to understand Ashbery. His work was so elusive and difficult that people who talked authoritatively about it were held in universally high regard.

"Ashbery?" said Miss Bishop. "Oh, no, we can't read Ashbery. I wouldn't know what to say about him."

"Couldn't we try an early book?" the student said.

"No, no. Let's try someone else."

"What about Auden?" another student asked.

"Oh, I love Auden, but we can't do him."

"Why not?"

"We just read him in my other class. We should read new people."

She acted as if we knew exactly what authors she had assigned the previous semester. I felt at ease. At least she was disorganized. I didn't have to revise my stereotype of poets entirely.

That first session must have seemed particularly unpromising. By the second class, the dozen original students had dwindled down to five—four undergraduates and me. The administration responded by moving us into a more intimate facility—the "seminar room" in the basement of Kirkland House. One entered by finding a well-hidden side door in one of the dormitory's wings, descending several staircases, and then wandering about until one came upon a vast, colorless room full of unwanted furniture and dismembered bicycles. There were pipes on the ceiling, and an endless Ping-Pong game went on behind a thin partition. In one corner stood a table slightly larger than a card table, and that was the only usable table in the place. Eventually, we all found the room, and the six of us took our places facing one another across the tiny surface.

"I'm not a very good teacher," Miss Bishop began. "So to make sure you learn something in this class I am going to ask each of you to memorize at least ten lines a week from one of the poets we are reading." Had she announced that we were all required to attend class in sackcloth and ashes, the undergraduates could not have looked more horrified. This was the twentieth century, the age of criticism.

"Memorize poems?" someone asked. "But why?"

"So that you'll learn something in spite of me."

People exchanged knowing glances, as if to say, "We're dealing with a real oddball." But the subject was closed.

Her modesty was entirely sincere. She was the most self-effacing writer I have ever met. She had her own opinions and preferences, but there was no false pride in her. Several times in almost every class, she would throw up her hands and say, "I have no idea what this line means. Can anybody figure it out?" And all of us would then scuffle ineffectually to her rescue.

Teaching did not come naturally to her. She was almost sixty when she became an instructor at Harvard, and one could sense how uneasy she felt in the role. She would not lecture to us, even informally. Sessions with her were not so much classes as conversations. She would ask someone to read a poem aloud. If it was a long poem, then each of us would read a stanza in turn. (At times, it reminded me of a reading class in grammar school.) Then we would talk about the poem line by line in a relaxed, unorganized way. She rarely made an attempt to summarize any observations at the end of discussions. She enjoyed pointing out the particulars of each poem, not generalizing about it, and she insisted that we understand every individual word, even if we had no idea what the poem was about as a whole. "Use the dictionary," she said once. "It's better than the critics."

She had no system in approaching poems, and her practice of close reading had little in common with the disciplines of New Criticism. She did not attempt to tie the details of a poem together into a tight structure. She would have found that notion unappealing. Nor did she see poems in any strict historical perspective. Good poems existed for her in a sort of eternal present. Studying poetry with her was a leisurely process. The order of the words in the poem was the only agenda, and we would go from word to word, from line to line, as if we had all the time in the world. We only read poems she liked, and it was a pleasure at Harvard to have a teacher who, however baffled she might be in managing her class, clearly enjoyed the things she was talking about.

We began with poems from "Spring and All," by William Carlos Williams. We worked through each poem as slowly as if it had been written in a foreign language, and Miss Bishop provided a detailed commentary: biographical information, publication dates, geographical facts, and personal anecdotes about her meetings with the poet. She particularly admired the passage with which Williams opened the title poem of "Spring and All":

By the road to the contagious hospital
under the surge of the blue
mottled clouds driven from the
northeast—a cold wind. Beyond, the
waste of broad, muddy fields
brown with dried weeds, standing
        and fallen

patches of standing water
the scattering of tall trees

All along the road the reddish
purplish, forked, upstanding, twiggy
stuff of bushes and small trees
with dead, brown leaves under them
leafless vines.

It took us about an hour to work through this straightforward passage, not because Miss Bishop had any thesis to prove but because it reminded her of so many things—wildflowers, New Jersey, the medical profession, modern painting. Her remarks often went beyond the point at hand, but frequently she made some phrase or passage we might have overlooked in the poem come alive through a brilliant, unexpected observation. For example, later in the poem Williams has four lines about plants coming up in the early spring:

They enter the new world naked,
cold, uncertain of all
save that they enter. All about them
the cold, familiar wind

"Williams is using a human metaphor for the plants," Miss Bishop explained. "As a doctor, he specialized in obstetrics, and here he sees the plants as if they were babies being born."

The poem of Williams' that she enjoyed talking about most was "The Sea-Elephant," which begins:

Trundled from
the strangeness of the sea—
a kind of
heaven—

Ladies and Gentlemen!
The greatest
sea-monster ever exhibited
alive

the gigantic
sea-elephant! O wallow
of flesh where
are

there fish enough for
that
appetite stupidity
cannot lessen?

One thing she found particularly fascinating about the poem was the way Williams made transitions. The poem moves quickly from one voice to the next, from one mood to another. It switches effortlessly from wonder to pathos, then to burlesque, and then back to wonder.

I think this was the side of Williams' work closest to Bishop's own poetry. She, too, was a master of swift, unexpected transitions, and her poems move as surprisingly from amusement to wonder, from quiet pathos to joy. But with "The Sea-Elephant" the subject alone was enough to light up her interest. She loved talking about exotic animals or flowers, and, not surprisingly, she proved formidably well informed about sea elephants. And she admitted that for her the high point of the poem was the word that Williams invented to imitate the sea elephant's roar: "Blouaugh." It was music to her ears.

We began reading Wallace Stevens' work, and started with "The Man on the Dump." Here, too, I think the choice was revealing. She often named the poets who influenced her most as George Herbert, Gerard Manley Hopkins, Marianne Moore, and Stevens, and a poem like "The Man on the Dump" represents the side of Stevens' work most like her own. While the poem is pure Stevens in its central concerns, it is slightly uncharacteristic in style. The rhythms are freer and more unpredictable than the blank-verse poems it superficially resembles. The tone is wry and quiet, the organization smooth and conversational, not pseudo-dramatic. The catalogues of rubbish and flowers it contains are more typical of Bishop than of Stevens:

> . . . Days pass like papers from a press.
> The bouquets come here in the papers. So the sun,
> And so the moon, both come, and the janitor's poems
> Of every day, the wrapper on the can of pears,
> The cat in the paper-bag, the corset, the box
> From Esthonia: the tiger chest, for tea.

Miss Bishop was more interested in Stevens' music than his philosophy, and she became most animated in discussing poems that bordered on inspired nonsense verse, where meaning was secondary to sound. She not only felt uncomfortable analyzing Stevens' ideas, she didn't even enjoy his more abstract works. Paging through Stevens' *Collected Poems* one afternoon, trying to figure out the next week's reading list, she claimed she wouldn't assign us a long, speculative poem, "The Comedian as the Letter C," because she couldn't stand to read it another time.

The only poem she specifically ordered us to memorize was Stevens' "The Emperor of Ice-Cream," and the next week she sat patiently through five stumbling recitations before leading us into a long discussion. Characteristically, she wanted us to memorize the poem before we talked about its meaning. To her, the images and the music of the lines were primary. If we comprehended the sound, eventually we would understand the sense. I also suspect that she stressed memorization in her class because it was one of the ways she herself approached poems. She knew dozens of Stevens' poems by heart and would quote them casually in conversation. She recited them like universally known maxims any of us might have brought up had we only thought of them first. Once, during a conversation on how Stevens used flowers, her face suddenly brightened and she said:

There are no bears among the roses,
Only a negress who supposes
Things false and wrong

About the lantern of the beauty
Who walks, there, as a farewell duty,
Walks long and long.

The pity that her pious egress
Should fill the vigil of a negress
With heat so strong!

Dana Gioia >>>><<<< 211

It was a moment of joy. Catching us all by surprise, the poem left us with the feeling of wonder that poetry should, but so rarely is allowed, to evoke. The conversation stopped, and we all sat around the table smiling like idiots. Miss Bishop was delighted at our reaction but also shocked to learn that none of us knew the poem. (She was always genuinely shocked to find that we did not know as much as she did about poetry.) Someone asked the title of the poem. "I don't know!" she exclaimed. "'Bears and Roses,' I think." And then we all began paging through our books in search of it. Eventually, we found it— "The Virgin Carrying a Lantern."

To Miss Bishop, Stevens' greatest subject was not poetry, the supreme fiction. It was Florida, the supreme landscape. She introduced us to Stevens with a long discourse on Florida—"The state with the prettiest name," she said—and returned to the subject repeatedly, always with affection and enthusiasm. But in a strange way her memories of Florida had become as Platonic an ideal as Stevens' visions of order at Key West. She was painfully aware of how much of *her* Florida had vanished. Her comments on Key West were always prefaced with disclaimers like "Back in the thirties, there used to be…" She spoke of it as if she were Eve remembering Eden.

"More delicate than the historians' are the mapmakers' colors," she once wrote, and, appropriately, she began her discussion of Key West with a topographical fact. "Key West," she told us, "is only ninety miles from Cuba." (Writing this down in my classroom notes, I, who had never been south of Washington, D.C., had marvelous visions of the Old South slipping mysteriously into Latin America in landscapes framed by Spanish moss.) Later, in discussing "The Emperor of Ice-Cream," she explained, "In the Depression, the town was one-third Cuban, one-third black, and one-third everything else." There were labor troubles, too, she said, and the cigar factories moved to Tampa. The town was full of unemployed cigar rollers. Cubans sold ice cream on the streets. People still used oil lamps. The poem was inspired, she maintained, by a funeral Stevens saw in Key West. Her explanation was the very antithesis of New Criticism. It was, in fact, the very stuff of apocrypha, but she convinced me.

She also told us in detail how Stevens went to Key West every winter with his friend and business associate Judge Arthur Powell. She even knew the hotel they stayed at—the Casa Marina. Much to our delight, she also told us, in disapproving tones, how, in 1936, Ernest Hemingway had beaten up Wallace Stevens once in Key West. It was, she informed us, Stevens' fault. He was drunk and had come up to Hemingway's wife (and Miss Bishop's friend), Pauline, and made an insulting comment about her clothes, which, we were further informed, "were perfectly respectable for a resort." Hemingway knocked Stevens flat. Miss Bishop spoke of the incident authoritatively and in great detail, as if she had been present. Perhaps she had. I later checked up on the incident, which seemed too colorful to be true, and found that it had really happened, though not exactly the way she described it. Stevens had actually insulted Pauline's sister, Ursula.

Miss Bishop disliked literary criticism. In 1950, she wrote for John Ciardi's anthology *Mid-Century American Poets*:

> The analysis of poetry is growing more and more pretentious and deadly. After a session with a few of the highbrow magazines one doesn't want to look at a poem for weeks, much less start writing one.... This does not mean that I am opposed to all close analysis and criticism. But I am opposed to making poetry monstrous or boring and proceeding to talk the very life out of it.

Twenty-five years later, her attitudes had only hardened on this subject. New Criticism was not only boring but misleading. She felt that most criticism reduced poems to ideas, and that the splendid particularity of an individual poem got lost in the process. A poem (if it was any good) could speak for itself. When she criticized the critics, she never spoke abstractly of "literary criticism," as if it were some branch of knowledge. Instead, she personalized the nemesis by referring collectively to "the critics," a sort of fumbling conspiracy of well-meaning idiots with access to printing presses. "They" were always mentioned in a kindly, disparaging way and dismissed with a single, elegant flip of her cigarette-holding hand.

Not dogmatic about her own theories, Miss Bishop did make a few exceptions: There were critics whom we were allowed to read without danger. "Allowed," however, is too weak a word, because when she liked a critic's work she liked it as intensely as the poems it talked about. Her favorite critic was her friend Randall Jarrell, who had been dead then for nearly ten years. His loss still seemed fresh, for she always spoke of him elegiacally, as if he had died only a few weeks before. Another critic she liked was Helen Vendler. She used Vendler's book *On Extended Wings*, about Stevens' longer poems, as a sort of Bible. Whenever we were to discuss one of the longer poems, she would bring Vendler's book to class. We would talk about the poem until the discussion reached an impasse, at which point Miss Bishop would suggest, "Now let's see what Vendler says." She would find chapter and verse, quote it, and only then let us go on.

I remember one rainy afternoon when a flu epidemic had decimated Cambridge. Only one other student besides me showed up for class, and the three of us sat around the table in the gloomy underworld of Kirkland House talking about "The Man with the Blue Guitar" and hearing the rain splatter against the basement windows. All of us were coughing from recent bouts with the flu, and especially Miss Bishop, who would still not stop smoking. She had, of course, brought her copy of *On Extended Wings*, and every few minutes she would stop the conversation to consult it. We would lean forward and wait for her to find the passage she wanted. Had a stranger suddenly been transported into the room, he would hardly have thought this was a seminar at Harvard University. It looked more like three old people in a rest home playing bridge with a dummy hand.

After Stevens, we moved on to Robert Lowell, and this switch gave us students an odd feeling of dislocation. Most of us were already familiar with at least some of Lowell's poetry, just as we had been with some of Stevens' and Williams'. But "Mr. Lowell," as Miss Bishop usually referred to him, was currently on the Harvard faculty. Some of us had had courses with him; all of us had met him, or, at least, heard him read his work. Miss Bishop had known him for nearly thirty years (they were introduced to each other by Randall Jarrell in 1946), and occasionally we would see them casually walking together near Harvard Square. Several of Lowell's poems were dedicated to her, and she had written the dust-jacket blurb for the first edition of *Life Studies*, reserved for us at the library. Now we were in Cambridge with her, reading Lowell's poems, living among the places and things he wrote about: the Boston Common, with Saint-Gaudens' monument to Colonel Shaw and his black regiment; the Charles River; the towns of Salem and Concord; Copley Square and Harvard University. All this gave Lowell's work a special immediacy. And if, twenty minutes or so into class, Miss Bishop slipped, as she sometimes did, and referred to "Mr. Lowell" as "Cal" we felt a thrill of complicity, as though she were sharing some secret with us.

Such slips were not common. She tried very hard to maintain a distance in discussing Lowell's poetry. While we students reveled in her occasional reminiscences, she sensed the incompatibility of talking about Lowell as a friend and trying to discuss his poetry objectively as a teacher. Consequently, Lowell was the only poet we studied about whom she did not spend a great deal of time filling us in with biographical information. Instead, she lavished odd bits of historical, literary, and geographical information on us as we read each poem. She was particularly thorough in explaining local references in Lowell's peotry. Whenever he mentioned a Boston neighborhood or landmark, she would immediately ask how many of us had been there. Anyone who had not was given a full description plus directions on how to get there. Being a transplanted Californian, I hardly knew Boston at all. Soon Miss Bishop had me spending my free afternoons tramping through the Common looking for Hooker's statue and searching out the swan boats in the Public Garden. And she was right in thinking that one could learn more about Lowell's poetry by spending an hour walking around the State House than by reading an article on *Lord Weary's Castle*. The author of *North & South, Questions of Travel*, and *Geography III* took local topography seriously.

What she commented most about in Lowell's *Life Studies* was his ability to turn a phrase that summoned up a time and place. In the opening poem of the *Life Studies* sequence, "My Last Afternoon with Uncle Devereux Winslow," she singled out certain phrases for special praise (my italics):

That's how I threw cold water
on my Mother and Father's
watery martini pipe dreams at Sunday dinner.

...My Great Aunt Sarah
was learning *Samson and Delilah.*
She *thundered on the keyboard of her dummy piano,*
with gauze curtains like a boudoir table...

...Aunt Sarah, risen like the phoenix
from her bed of *troublesome snacks and Tauchnitz classics.*

Lines like these would send her off on a flurry of memories and associations, and then she would speak of *Life Studies* as if it were her family album. Every poem seemed like some snapshot from her childhood. She made us realize that what was so extraordinary about these poems was not that they were confessional or technically innovative but, rather, that they re-created perfectly a small world that had passed away.

Occasionally, she spoke of her own family background, but always indirectly. She never mentioned people or events—only places and things. Once, she told us about a family heirloom she had inherited—a mediocre little landscape painted by a great uncle she never knew. It was only after owning it for some time, she claimed, that she suddenly recognized the place it depicted. Decades apart, both she and her uncle had seen and been struck by the same ordinary place—a "small backwater" in Nova Scotia. She transposed this incident into her "Poem," in *Geography III*, for her poetry almost always drew its inspiration directly from life.

When we reached the end of *Life Studies*, we came to "Skunk Hour," which bears the dedication "For Elizabeth Bishop." I knew that Lowell had claimed it was partly modeled on her poem "The Armadillo," but I had always wondered if there was something else behind the dedication. (This was back in the dark ages before Ian Hamilton's biography of Lowell.) Had she figured personally in any of the episodes the poem describes? I waited for her comments—she always explained dedications to us. But this dedication she skipped over, so I decided to be bold and ask her.

"Oh, yes, it is dedicated to me, isn't it?" she said. "I really can't remember why. I'm sure he had a reason. I think it was because one summer when I was visiting him up in Castine—that's up in Maine—

we heard some noises out in the backyard, and when we looked we saw a family of skunks going through the garbage. He must have remembered I was there that night."

This explanation was hardly the revelation I had hoped for, but I sat there and pretended to be satisfied. The class continued, and for once she took us firmly in hand and began a splendid reading of the poem with hardly a word or comment wasted. When she came to the sixth stanza, she talked about how cleverly Lowell worked a line from a song into the poem.

> A car radio bleats,
> "Love, O careless Love...." I hear
> my ill-spirit sob in each blood cell...

"Do you mean that's a real song?" someone asked.

Miss Bishop responded instantly with a look of polite horror which meant that someone had asked a stupid question. "You don't all know this song?" she asked.

We all shook our heads, and so there in the Kirkland House basement, with the pipes clanking overhead, she sang it to us in a gentle pianissimo.

Kirkland was one of Harvard's handsome neo-Georgian "river houses," situated near the Charles. The four undergraduates in the class lived in other river houses, close by, but Miss Bishop and I came from the opposite direction. Our class was so small and informal that we all left together, and unless I slipped out quickly the moment it ended, politeness dictated that Miss Bishop and I walk back toward Harvard Yard together. And politeness was a virtue nurtured in her seminar. Descending into the basement of Kirkland House after the horn-honking, shoulder-banging tumult of Harvard Square, one stepped back into a slower, more gracious world, in which no relationship was ever rushed or small courtesy hurried by. The frayed trappings of our subterranean salon, where those heating pipes were the only gilding on the ceiling and a faint smell from the rusty furnace occasionally mingled with our teacher's discreet cologne, could make this gentility seem hard-won, but here for a few hours each week decorum triumphed over décor. Each of us was addressed as "Mr." or "Miss," even the mildest expletives were deleted, and gentlemen were expected to open doors for ladies.

Unstated rules of etiquette are often the most inflexible. By holding the door for our instructor during our exodus from the Kirkland underworld, I tacitly agreed to accompany her to Harvard Yard. Likewise, I knew instinctively from the change in her voice as we rose blinking into the sober light of day that all talk of poetry was now expected to cease. At first, I thought that this sharp division between her professional and her social identities was simply another example of her unusual propriety. Not till much later did I realize how much Miss Bishop dreaded all literary conversation. Under duress, she might talk a little about poetry, but as soon as possible she would change the subject.

She once told me a story that epitomized her attitude. Northrop Frye, as the Norton Professor that year, was the guest of honor at a dinner party one night to which Miss Bishop was invited. She was embarrassed, she told me, because she hadn't read any of his books, and then was horrified to discover that she had been seated next to him at dinner. As the meal began, she leaned over to him and confessed, "I've never read any of your books." "Wonderful!" Frye replied, obviously relieved. They spent the rest of the evening chatting about Nova Scotia.

My difficulty in talking with her on our first after-class jaunts stemmed from the opposite problem. I had read all her books, and my admiration intimidated me. At first, my shyness and her formality provoked discussions mainly of a meteorological nature. Then, one afternoon, for no apparent reason (though perhaps some fortunate black cat crossed the path of my imagination), I mentioned that my mother, back in Los Angeles, was trying to breed Himalayan kittens. I was immediately besieged by detailed questions, and from that moment we never lacked for lively conversation. Our favorite topics were pets, flowers, fruit trees, church music, and travel, which usually took me to California and her, inevitably, to Brazil, where, she assured me, the orchids grew even on telephone lines. On rare occasions, we even talked about books. Soon we began stopping occasionally "for tea" at a nearby Russian restaurant, where we both invariably drank coffee.

As the semester progressed, the undergraduates grew openly impatient with Miss Bishop's singular ways. Their efforts at memorization became so halfhearted and their recitations so halting and resentful that in April this opprobrious requirement was quietly dropped. By then, this capitulation scarcely mattered to the unhappy few. English 285 was not the course they had hoped for, and outside class some of them had begun referring to it as "Studies in Elizabeth Bishop." One student, a bright, broad-shouldered member of the Crimson football squad, summed up their despair. "I could have taken Lowell's class," he groaned. "He's going to be in all the anthologies."

Morale was not helped by the long seminar paper due in late April. We were asked to choose any modern poet (except the three discussed in class) and write an introductory essay on his or her work. In class a few weeks before the papers were due, Miss Bishop asked us which poets we had selected. No one volunteered an immediate answer, but after further questioning she learned that none of the undergraduates had made up their minds and that I had chosen Georg Trakl, a modern Austrian poet, whose work was then almost unknown in America. After some discussion, she reluctantly agreed to my unorthodox topic but not before suggesting—politely, of course—that I had squeezed this foreigner into her course through a loophole. I knew then that I had better write a good paper. But my troubles had just begun. At the next session, all but one of the other students announced that they, too, were writing on foreign poets. Across the tiny table, I felt the cold heat of a long stare. It was the kind of look that director's call a "slow fuse"—a look like Oliver Hardy's glare the moment before he brains poor Stan Laurel and exclaims "Here's another fine mess you've gotten us into!" More merciful than Mr. Hardy, Miss Bishop let me off with only that stare, and, hopelessly outnumbered, acquiesced in our collective xenomania, but not before asking, "What's wrong with the English language?"

Ten days after I submitted my *opus magnum* on Trakl, I received an envelope from Miss Bishop containing my essay and a typed letter. Neither the letter nor the paper's title page bore a grade. Flipping through my essay, I saw that every page had dozens of corrections, queries, deletions, and suggestions in Miss Bishop's spidery hand. Some pages had obviously been worked over three times—once in blue ink, then in red, and, finally, in the proverbial blue pencil. In horror, I began reading marginal comments like "Awful expression," "Unnecessary phrase," "A mouthful," "Not in the dictionary"—most of which were followed by an exclamation point, as was her ubiquitous and incontrovertible "No!" An occasional "Better" or "Yes" (no exclamation point) did little to revive my self-confidence. I had been weighed in the balance and found wanting. Only then did I turn to the covering letter, which began:

Dear Mr. Gioia:

You'll see that I have made many, many small marks and suggestions on your paper, but this is really because it is very good, very well-expressed, and I'd just like it to be even *better*-expressed, and, here and there, to read more smoothly.

If this was indeed a "very good" paper, I wondered, what happened to the bad ones? Then I noticed that even her own covering letter bore half a dozen revisions. Looking back over my paper, I saw that all but three of the hundreds of marks concerned questions of style. Was there a better word? Was this phrase necessary? Was I using a literary word when an everyday one would do? "When in doubt," she wrote at the bottom of one especially profound page, "use the shorter word."

By this time, I had realized that, for all her fumbling disorganization, Miss Bishop had devised—or perhaps merely improvised—a way of teaching poetry which was fundamentally different from the manner conventionally professed in American universities. She never articulated her philosophy in class, but she practiced it so consistently that it is easy—especially now, a decade later—to see what she was doing. She wanted us to see poems, not ideas. Poetry was the particular way the world could be talked about only in verse, and here, as one of her fellow-Canadians once said, the medium was the message. One did not interpret poetry; one experienced it. Showing us how to experience it clearly, intensely, and, above all, directly was the substance of her teaching. One did not need a sophisticated theory. One needed only intelligence, intuition, and a good dictionary. There was no subtext, only the text. A painter among Platonists, she preferred observation to analysis, and poems to poetry.

Our final examination surprised even me. A take-home test, it ran a full typed page (covered with the hand-scrawled corrections that by now were her trademark) and posed us four tasks unlike any we had ever seen on a college English exam. Furthermore, we were given exact word lengths and citation requirements, as well as this admonition as a headline: "Use only your books of poems and a dictionary; please do not consult each other."

First, the final asked us to "find, and write out, for each of our three poets, two examples of: simile, metaphor, metonymy, oxymoron, synesthesia." That seemed odd but easy. Second, we were asked to reread Williams' "The Descent" and answer a number of questions about what particular phrases meant as well as to find parallel passages in Lowell and Stevens. Third, we were asked to "paraphrase Lowell's 'Skunk Hour' as simply as possible, first giving the *story*, what is happening in each stanza: who, when, where," and then to answer a battery of questions about particular persons, places, times, and phrases in the poem. "Be brief!" Miss Bishop had scrawled at the end of her two paragraphs of instructions for this question. These questions were unusual but not altogether unexpected, since they reflected her classroom method. It was Question No. 4 that left everyone at a loss:

> Now please try your hand at 24 lines of original verse; three poems of eight lines each, in imitation of the three poets studied, in their styles and typical of them. (In the case of Lowell, the style of *Lord Weary's Castle*.) I don't expect these pastiches to be great poetry!—but try to imitate (or parody if you prefer) the characteristic subject-matter, meter, imagery, and rhyme (if appropriate).

We may not have consulted each other about the answers to this test, but, walking out of Kirkland after the last class with the final in our hands, we could not help talking about the questions. Miss Bishop had gone off to her office, and we were alone.

"I can't believe it," one of the undergraduates moaned. "We have to write poems."

Someone else offered the consolation that at least everything else on the exam was easy.

"Yeah, but we still have to write poems."

Later that week, turning in my final exam, at Miss Bishop's office, I stopped to visit her one last time before I left for California. A student's farewell to a favorite teacher is usually a somber ritual, and I approached this occasion with the requisite melancholy. Entering her office, I wondered if I would ever see her again.

She seemed glad to see me. Indeed, she appeared generally more cheerful and carefree than I had seen her in weeks. She launched immediately into uncharacteristically lighthearted chatter, against which my youthful solemnity proved an inadequate defense. We talked for almost an hour. She even asked for my California address—that meant there would be letters. I enjoyed the visit but was slightly puzzled nonetheless. I had never seen her so animated. It was only as I rose to leave that I understood. More than any of her students, she was overjoyed that classes were over.

The Litany

This is a litany of lost things,
a canon of possessions dispossessed,
a photograph, an old address, a key.
It is a list of words to memorize
or to forget—of *amo, amas, amat,*
the conjugations of a dead tongue
in which the final sentence has been spoken.

This is the liturgy of rain,
falling on mountain, field, and ocean—
indifferent, anonymous, complete—
of water infinitesimally slow,
sifting through rock, pooling in darkness,
gathering in springs, then rising without our agency,
only to dissolve in mist or cloud or dew.

This is a prayer to unbelief,
to candles guttering and darkness undivided,
to incense drifting into emptiness.
It is the smile of a stone madonna
and the silent fury of the consecrated wine,
a benediction on the death of a young god,
brave and beautiful, rotting on a tree.

This is a litany to earth and ashes,
to the dust of roads and vacant rooms,
to the fine silt circling in a shaft of sun,
settling indifferently on books and beds.

This is a prayer to praise what we become,
"Dust thou art, to dust thou shalt return."
Savor its taste—the bitterness of earth and ashes.

This is a prayer, inchoate and unfinished,
for you, my love, my loss, my lesion,
a rosary of words to count out time's
illusions, all the minutes, hours, days
the calendar compounds as if the past
existed somewhere—like an inheritance
still waiting to be claimed.

Until at last it is our litany, *mon vieux*,
my reader, my voyeur, as if the mist
steaming from the gorge, this pure paradox,
the shattered river rising as it falls—
splintering the light, swirling it skyward,
neither transparent nor opaque but luminous,
even as it vanishes—were not our life.

THE EDITORS

LEE MARTIN is the author of a collection of stories, *The Least You Need to Know* (Sarabande, 1996); a memoir, *From Our House*, (Dutton, 2000); and a novel, *Just Enough Haughty* (Dutton, forthcoming). Stories and essays have appeared in such journals as *Story, The Georgia Review, DoubleTake, Glimmer Train, Creative Nonfiction, Shenandoah,* and *New England Review*. He teaches in the creative writing program at the University of North Texas where he also edits the *American Literary Review*. He is a recipient of a creative writing fellowship from the National Endowment for the Arts.

JEFFREY SKINNER is currently Director of Creative Writing at the University of Louisville. His published collections of poetry include *The Company of Heaven* (University of Pittsburgh Press, 1992), *Late Stars* (Wesleyan University Press, 1985), and *A Guide to Forgetting* (Graywolf Press, 1988), which was a National Poetry Series selection. He is the recipient of grants from the National Endowment for the Arts, the Howard Foundation, the Ingram Merrill Foundation, and the Kentucky Arts Council. His poems appear regularly in such publications as *The Atlantic Monthly, The New Yorker, The Nation,* and *The Georgia Review*.

ACKNOWLEDGMENTS

PHOTO CREDITS

Michael Collier (page 1) by Lorin Klaris Photography

Jay McInerney (page 13) by Mary Entrekin

Tess Gallagher (page 37) by Tim Crosby

David Huddle (page 49) by Marion Ettlinger

Reginald Shepherd (page 77) by Robert Giard

Elizabeth Graver (page 123) by Debi Milligan

Sylvia Watanabe (page 151) by W. P. Osborn

David Wojahn (page 171) by Michael Trombley

Dana Gioia (page 201) by Star Black